One Silver Summer

One Silver Summer

rachel hickman

Old Barn Books

AN OLD BARN BOOK

Copyright

Published in the UK and Australia and New Zealand
by Old Barn Books Ltd, Warren Barn, West Sussex, RH20 JW, UK
www.oldbarnbooks.com

Rachel Hi... has ... the right, Designs
and Paten... ... ed as the author of this work.

Published by arrangement with Scholastic Inc.,
Broadway, New York, NY 10012, USA

Cover design and artwork by Helen Crawford-White
Typesetting and text layout by Eyelevel Design
Printed and bound in Great Britain by CPI Group (UK) Ltd,
Croydon, CR0 4YY
The paper used in this Old Barn book is made from wood grown
in sustainable forests.

First UK edition
Distributed in the UK by Bounce Sales & Marketing Ltd and
in Australia and New Zealand by Walker Books Australia

ISBN 9781910646298
Ebook ISBN 9781910646267

For my family

"Why is summer mist romantic and autumn mist just sad?"
— Dodie Smith, *I Capture the Castle*

"You understand now ... how simple life becomes when things like mirrors are forgotten."
— Daphne du Maurier, *Frenchman's Creek*

1

ALEXANDER

Alex squared his shoulders in the hand-me-down, black tail-coat that tugged across his back because he was broader than his father. He loosened his white tie and too-tight collar and ran a hand through his dishevelled hair, still damp from the shower. He was dreading the party below him.

Music poured in from the main hall and a shriek of laughter carried up the great staircase, hairspray meeting the whiff of old sports kit.

So this was it, the Summer Ball. The one night a year when the girls from across the river were allowed inside these ancient boys' school walls. At the foot of the stairs, Alex could see Plum waiting, pretending that she wasn't, ruffling her hair and laughing too obviously with her friends. Plum Benoist. *Ben wah.* Her name sounded like the air kiss that would soon skim past his ear. He knew why the best-looking girl at the ball was standing there, and it had nothing to do with him. Not the real him.

Alex wished he could clear his head, but a jumble of thoughts kept going around and around. What he'd learned from the reporter with the hard red smile who'd stalked him from the riverbank that day: "Alexander, is your mother heartbroken at the split with your father?" He'd stopped rowing, the boat rocking a little as a jolt of pain passed through him. The anger came later, when his father called him. Too late. His son should've been told first, before it got out. Was it really so hard for his parents to remember him?

So there he was now, hands in his pockets, scuffing his way down, expected to carry on and pretend that nothing was wrong. So bloody British. With every step, he could feel the eyes of the crowd below. The girls fluttered like moths as Plum stepped into the light to meet him. Her hair smelled of perfume and her grip was small and vice-like.

"At last." She blinked up at him, her lashes sweeping the room behind his back. "Come on, let's dance before we get surrounded."

"I don't feel like..."

Almond eyes took him in, narrowing slightly. They glinted like a cat's, as if to say he should be pleased that she'd waited. And he was, he supposed. His mate Gully winked at him from a doorway. No help there. Alex glanced at Plum again, took a deep breath, and kept it together. She looked amazing. And she was rescuing him from himself, which was a good thing. Brooding never got him anywhere.

"Okay, why not? I like this song." Music was his escape, along with rowing. Only riding a horse was better than the reach and dip of oars, and the run of a boat over water.

"Oh?" Plum wasn't listening. "What's playing? I hadn't noticed." She swished her hair.

Alex looked down at her. Her skin was flawless, unless it was her make-up. Blonde hair fell about her shoulders and a slight smile flitted on her lips as everyone parted to let them through. Alex could almost hear the murmurs as he shunted her clumsily towards the darker edges of the dance floor and pulled her closer than he intended. From the corner of his eye, a master stepped forward, saw it was Alex, and stepped back.

"Feeling better now?" Plum asked, her mouth so close to his ear that the music stuttered.

"Yeah. Sorry I was late." He made a bigger effort to speak. "Parent stuff, you know?"

Plum had been there when that reporter screeched across the water. The first girl to ever steer the First VIII boat since their cox got suspended.

"Divorce," she said with a knowing smile. "You get used to it, and there is an upside, you know?"

"What's that?"

"You can ask them for almost anything, and —" she looked up and locked eyes — "you can confide in me."

Arms around his neck, she wriggled closer. Did she expect him to kiss her in front of everyone? He took a clumsy step back, hitting a wall. It would be so easy to give in, body

3

over brain. He could feel the heat of her skin and the bones of her hips ... and yet it didn't feel right. He swallowed. It was too public. And just ... wrong.

As the clock struck midnight, the girls piled back on their coach. Plum was the last, and Alex still hadn't made a move, so she leaned up and kissed him instead, to a chorus of wolf whistles. Surprised, he didn't close his eyes, and all he remembered later were the blinding flashes from the cameras camped at the school gates.

It was as if he'd mistakenly stumbled on a stage and the audience had clapped. Back in his study bedroom, he didn't bother to change, but slumped on his bed with his whole world spinning. How could he face them all tomorrow? He couldn't stand another minute in this place. The ball had been the final straw. People might dream of sending their sons here, but for him it was all wrong. The pressure to be someone he wasn't. Pressure to impress. Pressure to stand out. Pressure to be smarter, row faster, pass the ball, hit a six...

He sat up and swung his legs to the floor. Why didn't he just go? Get up and walk out before term ended? Find his own way home. He could already hear the sea in his ears.

2

SASKIA

Panic seized Sass like a hand to the back of her neck. Breathe, Sass. Breathe, Saskia reminded herself. She lifted her eyes to the horizon, where the sea and sky collided in a flat line of shadow. Her heart was already in pieces. The distance didn't help. Even three thousand miles from home, she could still hear the skid of tyres and a horn that went on for ever.

Ducking through a fence on the other side of the cliff path, she began to run away from the unfamiliar house full of sympathetic stares. She didn't care about the thistles and thorns that caught the backs of her legs. She barely even noticed the smudge of blood and sweat trickling down her left calf. She thought that if she stopped, she'd fall and slide all the way down the steep Cornish hillside into the cold blue sea, so she raced away, desperate to feel like herself again. A girl who, not three months ago, had trained for the swim team and dived from the uppermost board. Not the girl she was now, shivering by herself on the side.

Sass came to a standstill at a battered gate hanging off a dry-stone wall, blood pumping and breath ragged. She looked around, swiping at a cloud of insects near her head. Beyond the gate, a shaded tunnel of trees showed her a way through the fields ahead.

She was about to set off again when a sudden scuffle behind her made her jump and a panting scruff of black hurtled up.

It was her uncle David's dog, a terrier rescued from the pound not so long ago. He seemed super pleased to see her and was so black-eyed cute that she couldn't help smiling. She'd liked him from the first moment he'd jumped up at her, all four legs off the ground, his tail wagging like a crazy speedometer.

"Hey, Harry, come here, boy." She squatted down and held out a stale potato chip from her pocket. The dog lay down flat on his belly, legs out behind him, tongue lolling. He cocked his head as if to say, "Don't you speak Dog?" but then reached forward and sniffed her hand with his grey-speckled muzzle. Ever so gently, he took the chip, and Sass caught him by the collar. "Got you," she whispered.

And in that moment, Sass felt the pain ease just a little. Harry didn't keep asking if she was okay; his thumping tail said, "Get on with it, there's no other choice," and she liked that. It was honest. Truthful.

But he didn't do sitting. Or sadness. Not when there were rabbits and cowpats and foxes to sniff out. He wriggled from her grip and under the gate, his wet nose glued to the ground. Sass glanced down at the tarnished sign as she climbed over it: TRIST HOUSE ESTATE. KEEP OUT. NO TRESPASSING. Ever since she'd set foot in England, she'd been in someone's way. Well, she couldn't leave the dog, even if he was a runaway train down a bumpy track.

Harry slowed at last, zigzagging from tree trunk to burrow. Sass did the same, picking her way through the mud and the nettles. She was about as far from the city as you could get, stranded at the furthest westerly tip of England. All around her was silent except for the rustle of leaves.

Through the bowed trees ahead, the track channelled up to something that she couldn't quite make out. She squinted harder. The way ahead was blocked by a pair of tall arched doors set in a high brick wall. Were they carriage gates, as in a horse and carriage? Who, she wondered, had clattered through here in the past? She liked it when history peeked through paint cracks. If you looked closely, nothing ever disappeared. Even at home in New York there was hidden cool behind the shabbiest buildings. Like wearing vintage clothes instead of new. Whoever wore them before had lived between those stitches, their dreams and secrets held together by coloured threads. Sass pushed up the sleeves of her mom's old sweater. The smell of her had gone now and the bottom edge had begun to unravel, but she still wore it. Just because...

Beside the arched gates was an ivy-covered door. Sass rattled the old latch. It was locked. She rattled it again. There was no getting through. Disappointed, she picked up Harry, who was sniffing a plant that smelled a lot like garlic, and turned to head back. It was then, framed by a tangle of wild roses, that she saw the silver horse.

Sass peered through the thorns. Hugging Harry closer, she knelt down and shuffled up on her knees. In the half-light, the quiet meadow beyond was lush and green. A field of flowers turned to gold by a last burst of sun, the air heavy with the earthy scent of a forgotten wildness.

As a city girl, Sass didn't know much about horses, but she'd always felt sure that if she'd had the chance, she'd have liked them. When she was younger, she'd stuck a poster of a rearing black stallion on her wall, all flying mane and glossy tail, at the head of a herd of wild horses. This one was all on her own and she was a girl, Sass was sure of it. Shabby, covered in burrs and mud patches, shaking her head from flies. Made more beautiful for being real, standing there resting her back foot as she grazed in the shadows.

The silver horse raised her head, ears pricked. She gazed at Sass, her black eyes hopeful, before nodding her nose and going back to the grass, nibbling lips searching out the best dandelions and thistles. It was a moment of perfect stillness, like a kiss on the forehead, or the soft squeeze of a hand. Watching her, Sass felt like she'd met a friend.

An owl broke the silence, followed by Harry scrabbling to get down. Sass hung on, refusing to let go. In her stubbornness, she stumbled sideways and fell on her elbow. The horse flung up her head, wheeled around, and cantered away.

"Look what you did," she muttered in the dog's ear, rubbing her arm. "That hurt!"

A fat, wet droplet landed on her skin, followed by another. In a minute, it would pour. Sass looked up at the ever-darkening sky. What was it about this place? One minute a glimpse of magic, and then came the rain.

She got up, her arms covered in goosebumps, her back soon soaked by her hair. Tomorrow, she thought. Tomorrow, she promised herself. She'd come back and find the horse again, because however wet she was now, something warm and bright sheltered on the other side of that hedgerow.

3

TRIST

Alex got off the bus at the top of the hill and pulled his hood low. The air brakes of the number 37 hissed loudly as it rolled off down toward the village and disappeared between the tall hedgerows bordering the lane. It was the first and last time he'd ever take a bus. It took ages: no wonder people moaned. Glancing around, he crossed the road and ducked down an overgrown short cut.

Walking out had been unexpectedly easy. He wondered why he hadn't done it before. They'd catch up with him, no question, but perhaps he'd get a few more hours by himself. Alex looked at his watch: an old Rolex. The police were slow off the mark; his father would be less than impressed.

He kicked up a stone and it arced across his first view of the sea in months. *His* sea. Black and blue, under a scrum of cloud. So endless that Alex felt invisible. He grinned at last and let his shoulders relax. Head up, he breathed it in: tasted the salt on his tongue and in the air that clung to him like a second skin. A skin he felt good in.

He strode on as weeks of weariness drained from his legs, tugging at the hoodie he'd worn all day over his uniform, the only anonymous piece of kit in his wardrobe. He pulled out his school shirt, which had stuck to his back. His school tie was stuffed in a pocket. It was unlikely that he'd be spotted now; he was almost home. The sky was stirring with possibility, and somewhere under the cover of the trees ahead, an owl hooted.

Where the path forked between the beach and the old cart track up to the house, it began to rain, lightly at first, before chucking it down. Alex enjoyed the cool on his face, and for a moment thought about going for a swim, stripping off and diving into the cold sea and letting it wash over him, but it would only cause a bigger fuss. He was better off behind the walls of Trist, where he could forget about mobile phones and the photos that would be circulating like wildfire.

Half running now, he couldn't get to the back gates fast enough. As he rounded the next bend, he wasn't looking where he was going, and almost smacked straight into someone. *A girl.* He stopped dead and flattened himself in the shadow of a tree.

She hadn't noticed. Too busy peering through the hedge into the meadow. Who was she? What was she doing here? He scowled. Trespassing, that was for sure, in the one place that was his.

The girl crouched in a short, flimsy skirt with a baggy jumper that made it look like she wasn't wearing very much

11

except mucky red Converse on her feet. Her black tights had a snag in them that ran the length of one of her legs and her hair dripped like seaweed between her narrow shoulders. She was in his way, and worse, the terrier in her arms had spotted him. Dogs were never as stupid as their owners.

It yapped and wrestled to get down, but the girl wasn't having it. She hung on determinedly, falling on her arm with a swallowed cry. Alex almost stepped forward to help, but then stopped himself in time. The girl scrabbled up and started back down the path, muttering at the dog. An American. Probably some gawpy tourist with a camera.

He had other things to worry about. They'd have worked out where he'd gone; there was nowhere else he'd go. Alex felt the key to the side gate crushed in his palm. The door was right there. He could smell the garlic that grew near it. He looked around him one last time and put the key in the lock. A creak of the door and he was through. With a sigh, he slammed it shut behind him and leaned against it. Alone at last.

Sliding down on his heels, Alex took in the line of oaks in the distance, standing sentry to the most beautiful house for miles around. Trist. Haunting in her granite-faced sadness. This was where he belonged, where he could be himself, without worrying that he was falling short of what people wanted him to be. Who they needed him to be.

Here, he was free.

4

THE HORSE IN THE MEADOW

Sass woke early and burrowed under her duvet, safe from the screeching gulls outside. Pale sunlight filled the whitewashed studio above the boat-shed where her uncle David painted during the day and at night she slept. She was getting used to the smell of paint and turpentine, and didn't mind being on her own because, lying in the dark, it was easier to imagine she was back home in her room with her things. Not that the lights ever went out in New York: you could see the city from space. She lay there and mentally listed everything she used to listen to before she opened her eyes at home:

1. The rattle of the shutter on the deli across the street.
2. The honk of delivery trucks.
3. The neighbours upstairs stomping overhead.
4. The buzz of her phone on the floor.
5. Mom telling her she was late.

A weight on her feet stirred. Harry. Sass heard him jump down and begin sniffing at stuff. She'd have to get up and take him out because that was the deal for having him with her. Way to go, the easy life of a dog: eat, sleep, bark. With a sigh, she threw off her bedding, pulled on her only pair of jeans, and Mom's sweater, and went out.

The rain had stirred things up. Harry tugged her down the stone steps, past her uncle's cottage next to the studio, and on to the shore, where he lifted his leg against a pile of fishing nets and crab pots. After that, he snapped at the tide coming in until a wave broke over his head. She grinned when he shook himself dry in a shower of shiny drops.

A voice called out behind her.

"Morning, Sass. It's going to be beautiful today. Coffee?"

It was her uncle, leaning over the sea wall at the end of the small cottage terrace, holding out a steaming mug. He looked kind of crazy in his paint-splattered sweater with holes at the elbow, but there was something of Mom in his blue eyes, her eyes too, kind of intense in the way they creased up in the corners. Not that Mom and he were that alike: he was dark to her fair. Though she'd become a lot blonder over the past few years, covering the greys, she'd told Sass with a wink.

She hadn't been as straight about having a brother. Sass had figured out that her mother was maybe fifteen when her uncle David was born. Was that why they'd never been close?

"Yeah. Coffee's good. Thank you." She avoided his gaze, stepped up, and took the drink, sitting down on a rock with her back to the harbour wall. Running a finger around the chipped rim, she waited for it to cool, or for her uncle to say something else. Let him speak first. She wasn't about to spill her guts to this stranger with her mother's eyes.

After an age, he began carefully. "Were you all right yesterday evening? You came in soaked through."

Sass was ready to be polite, but not completely truthful. Not yet. "Yeah, fine, just tired, you know?"

"I didn't know you were going out."

Too many questions. She felt herself prickle. "I didn't know myself until I went."

"Still, tell me next time so I don't — worry." His voice trailed off and he looked up at the horizon. Sass followed his gaze: in the distance, a triangle of red sailed across the open sea beyond the tiny port. Her uncle was pointing at the water with a paint-stained finger. She could see he chewed his fingernails like she did.

"D'you know, Sass, the best thing about living near the ocean? It washes away the bad stuff. It's just going to take time, though, lots of time." There was a gruffness to his voice. He cleared his throat.

Sass's reply stuck in hers. Who was this man she hardly knew to tell her? He'd never visited them. He'd never even called, to the best of her knowledge.

"Listen, I'm driving over to the gallery if you want to come? There's some great stuff you might like to see?"

"No, thanks. Art's not my thing," she said, trying to ignore his disappointed face. She actually liked art, and the gallery looked kind of cool, a converted chapel that he'd pointed out on a trip to the store, but she couldn't handle any more awkward silences. "I'll stay here with Harry. I'm okay hanging out with him."

She crouched down and pulled at the dog's flopped ears. "Well, if you're sure? Things will get better when school starts. You'll be with kids your own age."

Sass picked up a handful of sand, scrunching it in her fist before letting it slip through her fingers. "Yeah, maybe." She hadn't been in touch with any of her friends since she'd arrived in England. You had to climb a mountain around here to be in the twenty-first century: no Wi-Fi, no cell signal, no money. Besides, no one, not even her best friend, Lauren, had known what to do after the accident, and after the first round of awkward hugs and promises to be there whenever she needed, they'd drifted thousands of miles apart. Maybe she'd write to her sometime when she was feeling better.

Her uncle was staring at her. Sass drained the last of her coffee. "You go," she said. "I'll take Harry for a walk. A long one. Over the top of the headland."

She stood up to show that she meant it. Uncle David rubbed the back of his head, as if undecided about the right thing to do. After a pause, he made up his mind.

"Okay. Your choice." He looked guilty, but Sass felt relief. "Want to know something else, Saskia?" He paused and smiled sadly.

She held her breath, her shoulders tense.

"You're so like her..." And before she could ask him what he meant, he touched her arm and left.

It was still early, and since the tide was out, Sass clambered over the rocks with Harry. The terrier got to splash through every pool and roll on washed-up dead fish because her mind was somewhere else. The horse from the meadow kept nudging her way in. There had been something magical about her: so still and silver in that field of flowers. She didn't know why exactly, but Sass wanted to see her again.

Harry led the way over the headland. At the top, Sass looked down at the village: a cluster of cottages clinging like barnacles to a coastline that stretched on forever. A screeching, black-headed gull moved her on, flapping too close to Sass's head, and she fled up the path. It was hotter already and the air seemed to shimmer around her.

Retracing her steps from the evening before, Sass came to the arched gateway and the hedgerow where she'd spotted the horse. She couldn't see much through the leafy green, but it was clear the animal was no longer nearby. Disappointed, she pushed at the gates, solid between their vine-covered posts. No way were they budging. She looked again at the ivy. Could she shimmy across? She'd always been good at climbing.

Sass tested her weight on the vines, which seemed to hold her. Pushing Harry through a small gap in the hedgerow below, she scrambled up and along, until she was right above

17

the meadow. She hung down and jumped the last few feet, calling to Harry, who was sniffing at a rabbit hole.

The paddock was just as she remembered, only more beautiful. Spindly-stemmed wildflowers with showerheads of tiny white petals grew up past her waist. There were wispy feather-like grasses glistening with dew, and behind her stretched tangles of thorny roses, hot pink and scented. The meadow sloped slightly downwards and she followed the incline to the bottom of the dip, where she saw the horse, just a few feet away, drinking at a creek.

An instinct told Sass not to walk straight up. She remembered how they'd been with her after the accident: careful, gentle … slow. She blotted out the memory of the crushed cans and cartons of milk spilled across the sidewalk. Offering her palm, she watched as the animal ambled over, ears pricked, to nuzzle her hand.

"Hey, I've got something for you." Sass held out a mint from her pocket. Soft lips took it, chewing and chomping messily, before nudging her for more.

"What about me, Greedy? That was my last one. See? All gone."

The horse looked old, with her ears twitching back and forth. Up close, Sass could see she was almost white, made silvery grey from a distance by a splatter of paint-like, black spots. Sass scratched behind the big horse's twitching ears and down her long neck, working at the knots in her mane.

The nearby creek looked tempting in the gathering heat and Harry was already drinking, his pink tongue lapping noisily.

Stooping, Sass cupped her hands in the clear water and drank too. It was good. She sat down and pulled off her uncle's wellington boots, and, with a sharp gasp, dipped her bare feet, wriggling her toes. She splashed her face, lifting her hair to enjoy a cool trickle down her neck. As she straightened up, Sass caught sight of something hidden behind an overhanging willow.

It was a wreck of some kind. She stood up and moved closer. An old horse trailer like a rusted tin can rested on a couple of musty hay bales. There were no windows to look through, but a low door at the front was held open by a straining striped tie? Sass's curiosity was pricked.

"Hello! Is anyone in there?" she called.

As her eyes adjusted to the dim light inside, Sass saw that someone had been there, and recently. Along with a stove and a scatter of spent matches was a horse blanket flung across an empty campbed still wearing the imprint of a body. A voice in her head told her to get out, but Sass had caught sight of a leather halter hanging on a nail. She reached up and took it down, turning it over in her hands. It was old and well oiled, stuck with white hairs, and there was a name inscribed on a brass tag: "BO" was all it said. What sort of name was that?

From outside, a voice cut the silence. "You!"

Sass spun around too fast and crashed straight into a boy with brown hair who'd stepped up behind her. They clung together in a kind of awful slow dance, tumbling out of the low door and onto the grass in a tussle of limbs, where Sass found herself looking down into a pair of very dark eyes. She gulped and slid off just as a canine cannonball shot out of the bushes.

"Harry, no!"

Her cry came too late as the dog tore into the boy's pants with a growl. Harry's target scrambled back in the mud, a shock of hair falling across his forehead. "Call him off me. Now!"

Sass jumped to her feet and grabbed Harry by the collar. "I'm so sorry, are your pants..."

"My *pants*?"

Sass flushed, suddenly recalling that pants meant underpants in England.

"I'm ... he's not mine. I ... Sass stuttered, but no way was the boy listening.

"You're not going to deny responsibility? Unbelievable!" A bite-size fabric tear flapped halfway up his thigh.

"Harry thought you were attacking me," she said, flaring at his stuck-up tone.

"What? *You're* the trespasser."

"Yeah, but you came up suddenly behind me and shouted!"

They were about the same age. Sass held his scrutiny. He reminded her of someone, but she couldn't think who.

"It wasn't Harry's fault. And you're okay, aren't you?"

Her gaze travelled down. She saw pale bare skin, but no blood. Angry Boy hadn't finished yet, fire in his eyes, his voice low and his English accent kind of icy. "That dog should be on a lead." He pushed his hair out of his face and took a step back, limping briefly as if he expected pain and it didn't come.

Harry knew his mistake, Sass could tell. The dog sat by her side, his jaws drooped, eyes innocently round.

The boy muttered under his breath — "Look, I just don't have time for this now. I'm sorry, but I'm in a rush."

"I'm sorry too," she replied, glad that at least they could go their own ways.

"What?" he spluttered. "I wasn't *apologising*." He stood up very tall and straight.

"Then why did you say sorry?"

"I was being courteous; it's a figure of speech."

Harry made a growly sound in his throat, sensing another fight. Sass bent to pick him up and forgot that the horse's halter was still hanging over her shoulder. It slipped down her arm and dangled there. She looked up, her bare toes curling guiltily. She had been messing with the boy's stuff — in his trailer.

"What were you going to do with that?" "Nothing! I wasn't stealing, I promise."

"Well, put it down. You're not allowed here. No one is, this is private property."

He looked down his straight nose at her, arching his eyebrows like she was expected to say or know something that she didn't. "Didn't you see the signs?" he asked.

"No!" she fibbed. There had only been the one that Harry had scooted under. If you didn't count a wall and barred gates.

"I'm sorry. I was walking the dog and saw her..." She pointed to the horse, who, despite the commotion, had come up to investigate and was now nibbling the boy's shoulder. "She's so beautiful that I followed her here, that's all."

The boy's gaze softened a fraction. Stupidly, Sass took it as a good sign and felt braver. "Is she yours? Does the horse belong to you?"

The glare was back, fiercer than ever. "No," he said quickly, "She belongs to the estate."

He worked here then, a stable boy. "And her name's Bo, right?" Sass waved the halter, letting it drop when she saw from the expression on his face that she was almost clapping like a seal.

"Look, you heard me. You need to *go*."

Sass fought the blush she could feel spreading up her neck. "Don't worry, I'm out of here!" Adding for extra measure, "I'm sorry to have wasted your so valuable time."

She pushed past him and called for Harry, who came when he was told for like the first time ever, and ran up the hillside.

This place: England. She didn't belong here. With all her heart, she wanted to go home.

5

THE PAINTING

Alex watched the girl go with a feeling like a concussion he couldn't shake off. Thank god she'd gone, although he wouldn't bet on not seeing her again. She'd left her man-sized boots by the creek.

The sound of a powerful car stopped him thinking any more about her. He straightened up and brushed himself off. They'd taken the best part of twenty-four hours to catch up with him. He watched with a hard knot in his stomach as minutes later, a black Range Rover and an accompanying police car appeared at the top of the meadow. Doors slammed and a tense group of muttering suits slid down the damp grass towards him.

"Bad night, sir?" His father's man, Fellowes, stepped forward: ex-army, ex-police, executioner, his eyes boiled eggs in a pork-pie face.

Alex rubbed his temple. "I'll get my things." What else could he say? He wasn't going to bleat about his parents.

The news of their break-up would be everywhere by now. Dissected, discussed, chewed over, until not even he knew what the truth was.

And soon there'd be photos of him too with Plum under some cheesy headline.

Alex ducked into the lead car, flanked by two police officers. He was a time waster, he knew it. These men had proper jobs. Criminals to catch. What was he, exactly? Fellowes answered — as if speaking for them all.

"The good news, Alexander —" he paused for maximum effect — "is that you're not going back until after summer. You're to stay here with your grandmother until your parents decide what to do with you."

He was warming up. A vein bulged above his left eye. Alex tried not to stare at it and failed.

"Nobody has the time for this. Do you have any idea of the worry and embarrassment you've caused? People lose their livelihoods when you go AWOL. Absent without leave. That's hardly fair, is it — in your position?"

Alex looked past him out of the window, conscious of not taking up too much space. He would apologise later. Bo was standing in the far corner of the field. Spooked by their arrival, she was almost blue-lit by the flashing lights. He'd make it up to her too.

As the car accelerated up the long drive to the place he called home, his heart beat faster. Trist House, the stern stone-faced nanny who had watched over the Tremayne family for more than three hundred years: births, deaths, fortunes and disasters.

When Sass got back to her uncle's cottage, grouchy and barefoot, the early sun had gone in and the wind had picked up. Looking down from the cliff path, she saw a woman she'd never seen before appear at the open kitchen window. She was standing by the sink humming as she put daisies in a jug, a scarf wrapped around her red-gold hair. After reading her mother's tatty Nancy Drew mysteries a few Christmases ago, Sass had wanted Titian hair. Nancy Drew looked up, put the flowers down, and came out the back door, wiping her hands on her jeans. Boyfriend jeans. She was barefoot too, but her toes were pinkly clean.

"Hi, I'm Jessie!" Her smile reached her green eyes, disarming Sass slightly.

"I'm Saskia," Sass replied, tucking a dirty foot behind her ankle.

"I know. I... work with David. I've been dying to meet you."

Gasping at her tactlessness, she flushed redder than her hair. "He's just coming now."

Not her uncle's girlfriend, then, but maybe an artist buddy? David came through the garden gate. "Jess, give me a hand with the painting, it's got to go up to the studio." He noticed his niece and stopped. "Hi, Sass, you're back too. Good."

Sass watched as they carried the elaborately swathed shape of a frame up to the boat-shed loft, the painting was wrapped in white muslin that billowed like a sail up the narrow stone steps. His studio. Her new bedroom.

"What is it?" she asked when they came back down. Jessie's eyes shining with excitement, strands of copper escaping their tie. "It's by Lucy Irving-Welch, not that David's let me see it yet. It belongs to the old countess up at Trist House."

"Trist." Sass mouthed the long "*s*" sound. Where had she heard or seen that name before? It sounded like a cross between "trust" and "risk". It sounded like a secret.

"Come on, David!" Jessie teased. "Can't we take a peek?" Her uncle wasn't to be persuaded. "You will, tomorrow, when we're ready to start work. It's stressful enough just having it here."

"Lady Helena won't mind," Jessie persisted, touching his arm. "She doesn't care what it's worth — everyone knows that."

"She will now," David said firmly. "Rumour has it the estate's for sale."

"What! For sale? They've lived there for generations. They belong there."

"Not any more. It's too much for the old lady and I reckon with the news, she needs the money. It's been a long time since the countess bred a winner."

"A winner?" Sass had been only half listening.

"Jump racer. All the money is in flat racing now. Dubai sheikhs and Russian billionaires."

"What are you talking about?" It was as if he was speaking in code.

"Horses, Sass! Thoroughbreds."

Oh. Sass thought about the grey horse. What sort of horse was she? Was Bo short for something, or just short? Short and sweet, and muddy. She smiled at the sudden image.

Much later that evening, while David walked Harry, Jessie got dinner ready. She knew where everything was, even the smallest things like pepper and ketchup, and Sass guessed from the stolen looks between the pair of them that the cottage was as much hers as his. For the second time that day, she felt out of place. The new kid at the party.

Sass went to bed early. Knees drawn up, she sat alone in the boat-shed, for even Harry had stayed with the others. She listened to the wind kicking up outside, trashing the waves, and felt a familiar rising dread. If there wasn't room for her here, where would she go?

Mom's funeral had been a blur. She'd been a black cloud waiting to break. They kept telling her she was in shock but not what that meant. Did it mean it was okay *not* to be choked up like everyone else? Could pain be measured in gulps? And why was it that when someone died, everyone wanted to bring you food when the recipe for Misery Pie was easy enough to make, just hard to swallow?

Take fifty bittersweet grown-ups. Mix them in your kitchen with a sprinkling of sugar and a handful of memories. Let the emotion whip up, beating in cream and vanilla hugs. Then when it's puffed up enough, stick the dish in the refrigerator, testing it with a knife every few hours. When everyone's left, it will be ready. Eat it on your own. Stone cold.

Turned out, the only family she had was Uncle David. He didn't know anyone either; he'd been away too long. But it was odd — all those people who loved her mother were happy for a stranger to take her daughter away.

At some point, Sass lay down, but it was a weird kind of sleep. She was by herself in a little boat lost at sea, being tossed in a mountainous ocean. Then at first light, when she couldn't hang on any longer, three white-foam horses with manes of crested waves rose up from the deep to rescue her and carry her home.

6

THE BOY ON THE BEACH

Alex leaned his chair back against the old range, eating his fourth piece of toast and marmalade. At his feet lay Susan the dog, with her chin on her paws, half blind now. The Labrador's legs were not what they once were, though her nose was as good as ever. She wasn't really his of course; she belonged to his grandmother. He hoped Grandma had understood why he'd come. Trist felt like home; none of the others came close and he knew she hated the stuff in the press as much as he did.

Predictably, his unexpected arrival hadn't impressed her, the staying out all night inexcusable. His 'needing head-space' had met with the frostiest glare.

"It wasn't fair. It wasn't clever. And it isn't done."

Two more police cars were waiting at the house when they'd swept in, neon yellow against old stone. Over the top, in his opinion. Grandma had dealt with it in her clipped voice that commanded attention. There had been mutterings behind closed doors and then that had been it. After the hundredth apology. Alex hadn't spoken to his Father yet, and wasn't going to, and who knew where Mother was. They were both keeping their heads down.

Separately.

Alex shoved his chair back and got up. He couldn't sit inside, not on his first day at home. Grabbing his coat, he went out. He needed air. He needed to ride.

He strode down to the yard, leaning into a wind blowing straight off the sea. Amy, his grandmother's groom, was sweeping Dancer's stable, pink-cheeked from mucking out.

"Weather's wild, sir, isn't it?"

She spoke so softly that Alex had to lean in to hear her.

"Err — It's just Alex, Amy." He felt himself redden. She knew that.

"You're not riding Dancer out in this? It's blowing a gale."

"I don't know. I haven't decided."

"Well, if you do, and I'm not saying you should, I can keep it secret. Promise." Her eyes were playful and she ran a finger across her lips, except they weren't zipped; they were slightly parted.

All right, then, he would. He might be in the doghouse, but he could do something useful like exercise the horse.

"If you get Dancer ready, I'll take him for a gallop. He'll need his martingale." He paused, not quite up to catching her eye, and murmured, "Thank you for looking after him while I've been away."

She bit her mouth and went off to get his tack. Amy was older than him, not by much, but she was the first girl he'd ever liked ... like that. They'd never done anything and, knowing his luck, never would.

Dancer was fresh. No way was he standing at the mounting block. He was practically cantering on the spot.

Amy held his stirrup while Alex swung himself up. "Be careful, won't you? He's pretty lively." She looked anxious now.

"Don't worry, we'll be fine. It's what we both need."

Alex headed for the beach, keeping Dancer collected all the way down, knowing the slightest easing of the rein would lose him. The wind seemed to howl through the trees and the waves pounded the rocks, the bay the weather's stage. When they reached the sand dunes, Dancer was on the edge of exploding. Energy surged through him. He shied and spooked, shaking his head and skittering sideways. Standing in his stirrups, Alex nudged the horse forward, a straight line of wet sand ahead. The horse leapt full tilt into a gallop, snatching the reins, foam flying from the bit as they raced ahead. And Alex felt his spirits soar.

Sass woke late to find Jessie and David in the studio with her, kneeling on the floor, unwrapping the painting from its gauzy layers.

"Sorry, my love, we didn't mean to wake you, but I —" Jessie smiled ruefully — "I couldn't wait."

The downside of a shared space. Sass sighed. Maybe she should pretend she was still half asleep, but Jessie was beckoning her to look. Sass yawned and sat up. Weirdly, this morning, things didn't seem as bad. They'd brought hot coffee and a breath of life, and Sass's nightmares had faded with the flying tails of the dream horses. Today, Jessie was okay, and David too. He looked younger with his morning stubble. Cool, even, in paint-smeared overalls. He didn't seem to own anything that wasn't covered in splatters.

The picture itself was turned away from her, its plain splintered back revealing nothing of what was on the other side. David heaved it up and turned it around on the easel, his body obscuring her view from the bed. Hugging the bedding to her, Sass scooched a little closer, rubbing her eyes when she saw it. It couldn't be? It was from her sea horses dream. Not exactly, of course, but close enough. She reached out and touched the furthest creature: the paint strokes were uncanny. In another time and another place, and perhaps in someone else's scared imagination, was a silver horse like hers. She traced a date and the artist's name with her finger: Lucy Irving-Welch, 1896. Should she tell Jessie or David about her dream? No. Better to keep crazy thoughts to herself. She thought of the leather halter with its brass name tag, and remembered where she'd heard, or rather seen, the name Trist before. Trist House: it had been stamped on the old sign, nailed to the field gate. The one that had said "KEEP OUT".

After Jessie and David left, Sass dressed quickly. Back at home, she might have waited in bed until Mom told her to get up. Now, as she pulled on her same old jeans, splitting at the knee, and a plaid shirt she'd found on a peg, she was aware that she had to think for herself. Jessie had picked up her laundry from the floor when Sass could have done it herself. She wasn't too fragile to help; it was just knowing when and how to.

David had taken Harry to the gallery, so Sass walked up the headland. She stood at the cliff edge looking out to sea, her hair whipping past her face.

Pier 11. The East River Ferry with Manhattan towering behind. Mom pointing and telling her that it wasn't far to the ocean. This ocean. Below her, Sass could see whitecapped waves buffeting the rocks, but before she could even blink, another memory tugged at her heart. It played out in her head until it hurt. The stab going to the core of her like a worm to an apple.

She closed her eyes and leaned forward, with only the gusting wind to keep her upright. A click of her heels and she'd be back there. There's no place like home. Sass had seen *The Wizard of Oz* on her eighth birthday. It was a really old movie but she'd loved it, especially Dorothy's sparkly red shoes — and Toto, who could forget him?

Mom had promised that a tornado couldn't really suck up an entire home and spit it out like a seed in another place. But that wasn't true. She spun around, dizzy with the pain, the full force of the salty air making it hard to breathe or open her eyes, and when she did, they were streaming. Everything led to the same ocean but the world hadn't shifted; just the people in it.

Sass flew down the coast path, head down in the wind, further than she'd ever gone before. After a mile or two, she came to a bay, a sweep of dark wet sand watched over by rocky cliffs on either side. And below her, galloping through the water, was a horse and rider. A flash of red and blue like something from a legend. So mesmerising that Sass had to stop and watch.

She followed the cliff path, until she saw a narrow short cut down. It wasn't much more than a parting in the bracken, most likely made by sheep, not people. Sitting down, she edged forward on her bum, feeling the rocky way with her toes. From the top of a steep outcrop, she could see that the horse had wheeled around and was now racing away from her, spooking at the wind and the waves. The rider, unaware of her watching from above, was crouched over his horse's neck. With a sudden whoop, he dropped his reins and stood in his stirrups, his arms outstretched, his horse straining forward, its mane and tail flying.

The animal was fine and lean, the colour of blackened steel. It moved with the lightness and speed of a racehorse – a charcoal slash across a creamy white page. When the rider reached the end of the beach, he sat down, half circled smoothly, and brought the horse back to a trot. Sass could see that the flash of red was the striped silk cover on a helmet with white stars and a blue bobble on top.

She peered over the edge, still ten feet or more above the beach, but instead of climbing back, she dropped down like a cat onto the soft sand beneath.

With a shock of recognition, she saw her mistake. A big one. The rider coming toward her was *him*: the boy from the meadow. She didn't have time to climb back. The beach was deep, but not especially wide, and as they were the only people on it, it was impossible to ignore each other. Sass half raised her hand, her stomach flipping. He'd think she was stalking him or something.

The boy gave her a curt nod and reined in his horse, which sidled to a halt. He corrected it with an impatient tap of his heels; it overreacted backwards in a cold splash of spray. "Whoa, boy!"

"You're wearing my flag!" Sass called out, hoping to sound casual, like she watched boys on horses all the time.

"I'm sorry, what did you say?" He bent forward slightly to hear her better.

"Um. Stars and stripes." She tapped her head to indicate his helmet, letting her hand drop as he raised his eyebrow.

"Actually, they're my colours as well." He patted his sweating animal and the reins slipped through his fingers to the buckle-end. The horse stretched forward, his nose butting Sass, who, grateful for the distraction, put a hand out to stroke the animal's neck, which was warm and damp, and sleek like a seal's.

"I guess he's not yours either?"

The boy studied her as if she were a crab who'd crawled out from under a rock. Sass glanced down just in time to see one scuttle across the sand.

"If only. He's going to be sold."

"So how come you're still riding him?"

"He has to be kept fit." The boy jumped down, looking more at home in worn breeches and long boots than Sass had ever felt in anything in her life, the silk on his helmet set back like a jockey's. Sass felt suddenly self-conscious in her ragged jeans and borrowed shirt. She stuck her hands in her pockets and dug a small hole with her toe that she wished she could disappear into.

"You know you're trespassing again."

What? Her discomfort turned to indignation. "Oh, I'm sorry! Is this your beach? I'd better go, then."

He gave her a strange look, took off his helmet, and ran a hand through his tousled hair. She noticed his taut forearm. His flattened back hair was kind of sweaty, which made her feel better. He loosened the belt around his horse's belly.

"What were you doing up there?" he asked. "Were you watching me?"

Get over yourself, Sass said in her head. "I didn't know it was you. I was sort of watching you both. He's a very beautiful horse."

"I see." He didn't say anything else, just sort of rocked on his heels, frowning.

With the wind loud in her ears, Sass couldn't tell if he was waiting for her to speak, or to leave. "So is this a summer job? Exercising horses?"

"Yes." He glanced away. "And you're on holiday, I suppose?"

He meant vacation ... it was hardly that, and Mom wasn't for sharing. Sass struggled until he spoke again.

"What do you think of Cornwall, then?"

"I don't know. I guess it's wild. It's kind of lonely — but I'm really into horses — It's a great — horse place."

The boy gave her a hard look, as if uncertain if she was serious then kicked a rock by his feet. "I never want to be anywhere else."

Like it was a confession, said with a forcefulness that made his horse jump too. It was a big horse. Sass took a step back.

"Sorry, I didn't mean to do that." Was he talking to her, or the animal? Or both? "You're from the States?" It was more of a statement than a question.

"Yeah. Brooklyn, New York, but I — I'm staying with my uncle in the village."

"Oh right, that's good..." He cast around him. "Well, I suppose I should show you the way out so the tide doesn't get you." He glanced back at her, and for a second, a shadow of a smile flickered at the corners of his mouth.

"Thank you. I didn't want to have to swim for it."

They walked up the beach, the horse jogging between them. Sass matched his stride, conscious of her hair blowing about her face. Hair a seabird might like to make a nest in. He took a short cut between some sand dunes to where the ground levelled out, and the coastal paths on either side of the cliffs came down to the beach, like two loose wires needing to be fused. This was where they would split. She would go right and he would head back to wherever.

"I'm Sass," she said, surprising herself. Blue eyes met brown with thick brows that knitted slightly.

"I'm — Alex," he replied carefully, as if not sure of his own name. "And this," he said, turning to rub his horse's forehead, "is the best horse in all of England. Bo's his mother. Remember the mare from the meadow?"

"Sure I do." Like she could forget. She reached out a hand to the animal's nose. "What's his name?"

"Sky Dancer."

Their fingers almost touched. "That's beautiful."

"Dave, for short."

"No way. You're kidding?"

He laughed out loud.

Sass felt her cheeks go pink, but inside she was smiling. Two could play at that. "What's so funny about Dave? My uncle's a David." She deadpanned.

"God," he said, looking mortified. "Is he really? I didn't mean to be rude."

"It's okay. It's fine, really! What's with you Brits? You're always apologising."

"Perhaps we've a lot to apologise for." He looked at her meaningfully and Sass wondered if he was thinking of their fight yesterday at the trailer.

She flushed. "No, really, you were right. I was — I admit it, most definitely trespassing."

Together, they walked as far as the footpath sign: a yellow arrow etched in wood. The boy . . . Alex, turned to her.

"Will you be all right from here? I mean walking back by yourself?"

"Sure, why wouldn't I be?" Sass laughed, but it came out sounding sharper than she meant. He was just being polite. She lifted her eyes to his. "I'll do my best not to trespass again. Although, it seems I can't help it." She smiled at him then. For real. Alex bit back a small grin and shuffled his feet. "I'll consider myself warned."

He clicked to his horse and strode off, leaving Sass unsure if she was happy or not to be on her own again.

7

THE COUNTESS OF TREMAYNE

Helena, Countess of Tremayne, stood in the tack room at Trist, cleaning saddles with her bucket and sponge. She leaned against the old wooden saddle horse and inhaled deeply. She adored the smell of saddle soap. She was wearing her favourite Hermès headscarf tied firmly under her chin, a woolly cardigan, and a pair of her grandson's tracksuit bottoms. Appearances and practicalities dealt with in one. She'd poached them from the washing; they were so extraordinarily comfortable. "Abercrombie and Fish", the label had said.

Still sprightly in her nineties, Helena had bred horses all her life, with an energy that mocked her age. Despite dozens of successful foals, she'd failed with her only child, Seraphina, Alexander's mother. It was all over the news. Nothing she loathed more than dirty linen aired in public. Her daughter was beautiful, but as flimsy as the designer frocks she wore. She'd made a marvellous match and produced Alexander, but the marriage had been a disaster. Now hounded by the press, she was looking at a divorce that would possibly cost her everything. And what of Alex? Pulled in all directions. Fresh air and exercise, that was what the boy needed. She just hoped this wasn't his last summer at Trist.

On cue, he wandered in.

"Hello, Grandma."

"I see you've been riding?" She knew, of course, he had. He was brighter. It had bucked him up no end.

"I couldn't stay in and do nothing. I expect I should've but I didn't." He regarded her steadily. "Dancer was amazing. You have kept him up to the mark."

Her grooms Figgy and Amy, had done well; stable work was hard, even with fewer horses.

"He is rather marvellous, but then his mother was a winner."

"Would you really sell him?" Alex's eyes rested heavily on hers.

"Darling, we'll see. I want you to keep him, but it's not my decision, it's your mother's, and she's not a country girl, is she? You really ought to talk to your father."

Alex's eyes slid away.

"But, Grandma, Dancer's yours and so is Trist. You should decide."

Helena sat down, her bones were aching. The thought of selling up was like a gin without tonic. Bitter. It was the horses she'd miss most, and the staff. Although apart from the grooms, they were almost as ancient as she was. Time they all went out to pasture. As for the house, so many memories, and not all of them happy. After all these years, she still felt like an outcast. It wasn't called Trist for nothing. Cornish for "sadness", there were plenty of tears and sighs caught up in these cobwebs.

Alex had picked up a sponge. Good grief, was he making amends for his disastrous arrival?

"Bo looks well. I didn't know you were going to turn her out in the field for the summer?"

Helena smiled; had he sensed her weariness?

"Bo needed a rest. Have you seen how grown up her foal in the pen is yet? Cheeky little madam. Didn't mind being weaned at all."

"No. I'll see her tomorrow. Have you thought of a name for her yet?"

Helena hadn't. Bo's foal had been born one freezing night in January before Alex went back to school. They'd come down in the morning and there she was, already woolly and shaky-legged beside her mother. Bo was old now and this filly would be her last.

"No, but I will. I always do. It takes time to find the right one."

8

PANCAKES AND SYRUP

Seagulls woke Sass, noisier than any alarm clock. She'd slept better than a caterpillar in a cocoon, and this morning she could feel the beginnings of butterfly wings. Seeing Alex galloping his horse through the surf had made her want to do something. For the first time in forever, she looked forward to the sun and wind on her face.

Sinking back against her pillow, she tried to imagine what it took to ride like he did, to gallop that fast. He was certainly brave, and nicer than she'd expected in a poker-faced sort of way. And best of all, he hadn't explicitly told her to stay away from the meadow. Not that she wanted to run into him again, but Bo was different; Sass wanted to see her.

She flopped onto her stomach and stirred her stuff on the floor with a finger. Most of her clothes were still in crates on a ship crossing the Atlantic, one of those long, dark outlines that slid across the horizon. She couldn't remember what was in

43

them. She'd brought the things that mattered most, the things you'd save in a fire. Her photo of Mom, safe under her pillow, along with Lion, the stuffed toy she still slept with because he was missing his whiskers and courage and she'd had him since she was two. Some of her swimming medals for freestyle and backstroke, and random bits and pieces: a Broadway ticket to *Matilda*, a lipstick of Mom's and some books, of course.

Harry was scratching to be let out. Still in her nightclothes, Sass took him down to the jetty. The tide was coming in, so they pottered above the cove, the dog sniffing at rabbit holes and growling at the lobster man checking his pots from a rowing boat near the shore. Sass decided on three new things:

1. To always walk Harry first thing in pyjamas because it felt good, so long as nobody saw her.
2. To get up and out and doing something.
3. To not get distracted by thoughts of boys with dark eyes. On *horses*, she added in her head, like that made it okay.

When she got back, Sass dressed and wandered into the kitchen, where David stood on his own, rinsing paintbrushes. Perching on the edge of the sink, Sass drummed her heels and poked at the dregs of paint swirling down the drain.

"Jessie not around?" she asked. Sass had noticed her bag of toiletries had gone that morning. David looked up, startled at her directness.

"She's at her place."

"But aren't you two —?" Sass didn't like to presume. "Aren't we what?"

"You know, living together? As a couple."

David took his time answering. He washed up and put the brushes in a jar on the windowsill. "Yes — and no. She has a life of her own, and I have you to think about now."

"I'm not in the way, am I?" Her newfound resolve wobbled. "You don't have to change things because of me — I mean, I really like Jessie." She pulled at a loose thread on her jeans.

"You're not in the way," her uncle said carefully. "Don't ever think that, but there's stuff that Jess and I need to work out." He paused. "But that's up to us. Right now, I'm about to make breakfast. Want some pancakes before I go to work?"

"Pancakes? Seriously?"

"Yeah, with syrup and bananas, like your mum used to make."

"You know about them?"

"Sure." He looked away for a second and then turned back and held her gaze. "She was my big sister. She used to make them for me."

David left for work and Sass cleaned up and took Harry out, letting the small dog rocket up the steep country lane to where it emerged from its cover of green. The pancakes and bananas had found a sweet spot inside her mind; wherever Harry decided to go, she'd follow.

Over breakfast, David had told her the story of his Cornish village. It was no bigger than a hamlet, he said, with its cluster of houses above high water, the same fishing cottages that had stood since the long-gone days of smuggling. Everyone had joined in it seemed: fishermen, blacksmiths, farmers and their families, because it was the only way to survive. When the wind, the moon and the tide were right, French brandy and lace were rowed ashore and stashed in caves and boat-sheds like her bedroom. They traded in danger to stay alive and ignored the inn on the hill. The Struggler's End, a grim reminder that anyone who got caught hanged at the end of a rope.

Halfway up the lane, Harry veered down a path to a stone stile. A new walk. Sass picked him up and climbed over, and found herself in a field of cows. Not the black and white female ones, wet-lipped with swinging udders. These were smaller, honey-coloured and doe-eyed. Calves but bigger. All baby boys, she thought. Some of them were lying down, while others chomped on the lush grass. There had to be at least twenty of them, and on seeing her, one of them began to low. It was so sweet. Or, it seemed sweet, until the solo moo became a collective mooing. When they scrambled to their feet, Sass felt the smallest trickle of apprehension down her back. They were much bigger than she'd guessed. And really curious; so curious that they were coming over now. A herd of teen bulls was charging her way. They were … galumphing towards her, or whatever it was that boy cows did before they grew into full-sized bulls.

"Shoo!" She shouted at the nearest one as she picked up Harry and held him close. The dog wasn't liking it either; she could feel him shaking. There were too many of them. The herd was jostling closer, crowding around and butting her like she was the most popular girl in the field.

"Stay calm and walk over here," an unexpected voice commanded. Sass risked a look over her shoulder. Alex was leaning over a nearby gatepost.

"I don't want them to come any closer."

"They won't hurt you."

"How do *I* know that?" The biggest bull was prodding her with his head. Not so cute any more. Her heart was thudding in her chest.

"Sass, listen. Wave your arms slowly and walk back towards me."

"I can't, I'm holding the dog."

"It's him that they're interested in."

"What do you mean?"

"Cows and loose dogs, they don't really mix."

"I didn't see any warning signs."

She ignored his rolling eyes.

Sass carefully made it over the gate to Alex, pleased when he ruffled Harry's head. She could feel her own hair bursting out of its rubber band like a firework and nettle rash ran down her legs. Before she left, she'd cut off her jeans, which was clearly a mistake. Worse, Alex had noticed, and her face went even redder when she saw that he was holding out a large, flat leaf.

"What's that?" she asked, doubtfully.

"It's a dock leaf. If you press it to your skin, it takes away the nettle sting."

"Oh? I never knew." Sass pressed it to her thigh. It seemed rude not to. She scraped her hair off her hot face. "Aren't you supposed to be at work?"

His turn to not meet her eyes. "I was on a break. Came up here to make a call. There's no signal down there." He tapped his iPhone. It was the latest one.

"Ah, okay."

"And you?"

"Just walking the dog. Again. Harry needs a lot of walking." "I know. I've got one too, a chocolate-brown Labrador. We've had her all my life. She's pretty doddery these days. She's sixteen, and all she wants to do is sleep."

"What's her name?" Sass liked the way his face softened when he talked about his dog.

"Susan."

"So English. Do you have a nickname for her too?"

He made a face. "Not usually —" adding with a hint of a grin, "she ought to be called 'Pig' because she steals food all the time."

The way he said *pig* made her unexpectedly giggle. "I see I've made you smile." Sass was about to apologize for her goof, when he gave a quiet but very definite, "Oink!"

Sass snorted – oh god, piggy style – and clapped a hand to her mouth. It was the relief of her rescue from Killer

Cows, that was all, and yet she couldn't seem to stop. She was a shook-up can of Coke: crying with laughter till she pressed a hand to her mouth to keep it still. So totally the wrong thing to do, but it felt ... *really* good.

Alex had never met a girl like her. Loads of girls giggled, then stared, or were loud and horsey, or perfectly cool like Plum, but she, Sass, seemed to have a way of knocking him off-balance and then making him feel ... good about it. If he took her fishing, he might end up happy just rowing in circles. So natural, he could almost believe she didn't recognise him. How was that possible, given who he was?

She wiped the palm of her hand across her eyes and nose, and surreptitiously down the back of her shorts. He pretended not to notice, distracted by her legs, which went all the way up to the curve of her bum, which of course was where all legs ended. He shook his head. She reminded him of a setter, a black-and-tan gun dog that he'd had on a shoot in Scotland last year, all wavy tail that kept getting in the way.

"Have you ridden yet today?" Sass was asking with a final effort.

"No, too much mucking out to be done. Dancer's out in his field. He's probably rolling right now in the muddiest patch he can find."

"How great to be a horse and just get down and wriggle in the dirt. It must be kind of satisfying."

There was something very real, believable and yet slightly breakable about her. Thumbprint shadows beneath the blue eyes.

"You're not used to the countryside, then?"

"No. I'm a city girl. I guess you've known dogs and horses — and farm animals — your whole life?"

"Pretty much." Cautious now... "I had a fat pony when I was five, called Magic. He'd stick his head down to eat and hey presto, I'd fall off." He smiled, thinking about Magic, but then felt the familiar trip switch whenever a conversation turned to him, which it almost inevitably did. He turned the subject back to her. "Do you ride, then? You said you liked horses."

"I like them, but I've never sat on one."

With her accent, her words rolled into one another, the way a wave gathered gravel on a beach, and Alex found he wanted to stop and listen.

"Sometimes downtown — in Manhattan, I saw trailers parked for the police horses. I always wondered where they went at night."

Part of him wanted to tell her about his last trip to New York, when he'd had the exact same thought about the horses queuing with their heads down outside Central Park. But what if she asked more questions? Where would they end? He wasn't going to mention the suite at The Plaza, or the round of receptions his parents had dragged him to. Better to say nothing at all.

"I could show you?" he said, jamming his phone in his pocket. What was he thinking of?

"You mean, teach me?" Her body a question mark.

"Yes. How to ride. We could meet in Bo's meadow tomorrow?"

"Oh," she said, with a hint of a smile that invited him in. "Yes — I'd like that."

"Well, then." He clasped his hands, twisting them hard. "I guess — I'll be seeing you again."

And a sort of static hung in the air, that made Alex think that if he reached out and touched her, he might light up inside.

9

TRUTH OR DARE

Sass stepped out of the shower and stood in the tiny, damp bathroom with a porthole for a window. Was today a date or a riding lesson? She wasn't sure. She hadn't been on many dates, not any that counted, and certainly not one like this. If it was one. She felt a flutter in her stomach.

Through the warm steam, she caught sight of her reflection in the small mirror on the wall. She rubbed at the glass with the edge of her towel and a smudged girl she half recognised looked back. Her face was still drawn, but not as pale as it had been. There were spots of colour in her cheeks and the sun had burned her nose. Same frown-y brows and that stupid freckle above her lip, but her eyes had a brightness in them that had been missing.

When she first met him, Alex had glared at her like something Harry might have dug up, but yesterday was different. Unless she'd imagined it? Maybe he was just being helpful to the crazy girl scared of cows? Hardly romantic. She smeared her face in the mirror. Just as well, since she had nothing to wear.

When she'd packed three months and six days ago, she hadn't been thinking about ... well, very much, except getting through the next hour.

She brushed her hair, tugging at the knots, before tying it up in the usual clump on top of her head. She'd risk a little mascara today. Crying was not an option. A spritz of perfume from a bottle on the shelf and she was ready for whatever came her way: date or lesson. Lesson or date. Dating lesson. Riding date. Which was it?

The locked gates to the meadow beckoned her like a thief. Even the bowed trees lining the old farm track ushered her up, cobwebs glistening on the dark-green ivy-covered gatepost that was her secret way in. On the other side, the morning mist was lifting, golden sunlight catching her as she ran down the slope. She slowed to a saunter when she saw that Alex had beaten her, and was sitting casually bareback on Bo. The horse was wearing her halter. Sass's heart bumped.

"Ah — there you are," he called.

He got down, swinging his leg over Bo's neck, showing off. The mare wasn't impressed and so Sass tried not to be either. He smiled and pushed his hair back from his forehead. It sprang forward. Untidy. Nice.

"You ready?" he asked with a slow grin. "Come over and I'll give you a leg up. Then I can hold her if she gallops off."

Sass gazed at Bo. Now that she was supposed to get on her, the horse had grown to the size of an elephant. "Am I really going to do this?" she whispered in the horse's soft black-tipped ear. As the mare butted her pockets, Sass leaned in to feel her warmth. "Please, please, please," she murmured. "Make me look good."

Alex cupped his hands, lacing his fingers to create a footrest, his feet planted on the ground. Today he was wearing old trainers and khaki breeches. Sass had kind of liked his long boots from before: black leather with a chestnut band around the top.

"Reach up with your left hand and grab a clump of mane. Then put your left foot in my hands and hop on."

Sass stepped up and a tremor ran through her, but she managed to follow his instructions and scramble onto Bo's back. Startled, the mare sprang forward, and Sass clung to her neck for balance as Alex pulled the horse gently around.

"Sit up, don't slump. And relax, she's not going anywhere."

"It doesn't feel like that!" Sass gasped.

"I promise, I've got her. Concentrate on sitting tight."

Bo might have been old, but she was light on her toes, and without waiting for a signal from Sass, she stepped out. Sass could feel every muscle in the horse's back ripple like water. It felt odd and wonderful. She was riding — almost.

"Don't grip too hard, just let your legs hang down." "But you said 'sit tight'?"

"I know" — he frowned briefly — "but what I meant to say is that if you want her to go forward, then all you have to do is squeeze with the insides of your calves. The rest of the time, sit still." He adjusted her ankle, his fingers brushing her bare skin. "Bo was a racehorse once."

"Really?" Sass's stomach did a loop.

"It was a long time ago, but she was a winner. The whole village turned out to welcome her home."

"I knew she was special." Sass felt brave enough to let go of Bo's mane and stroke her neck, still glad that Alex was at the end of the rope. As they navigated the meadow, he talked to the horse in a steady murmur that worked for Sass too. At the end, she slithered down none too gracefully, conscious of the nearness of his hand.

"Did you enjoy that?" he asked.

Could he not tell? Sass held her breath, time ticking in slow motion. She turned away as a rush of emotion threatened to shush her.

"It was perfect," she blurted, lifting her head.

His rare smile came out again and they walked back to the trailer with Sass leading Bo.

"You can take her headcollar off now."

"Okay, but show me slowly. I don't want to forget."

"Undo the throat strap first — see here?" He stood behind her. "Now stand with your shoulder under her chin and reach up."

Sass groped around Bo's ears.

"Pull the headpiece down gently." His hand closed over hers, the collar of his polo shirt at her neck. She could smell soap and mint . . . and hay. The halter came away and Bo swung off to graze. She'd done it. Lesson one, accomplished.

"You did well," Alex said.

"Thanks." She scanned his face for any sign of mockery, but he seemed sincere. "I should probably let you get back to work, I don't want to get you in trouble."

He ran his hand through his hair. A habit she could live with. "I have a few more minutes. I doubt anyone's missed me. Want to share this?" He took out a tangerine from his pocket.

They sat by the creek and split the fruit, its citrus sweetness sharpening the air as the morning slipped away faster than water from the moat of a sandcastle. Alex leaned back in the grass with his hands behind his head and closed his eyes with the sun on his face. Sass sat down cross-legged beside him and picked a dandelion clock. She blew on the gossamer-white seeds and watched as they spun in the air before floating down and settling on his chest.

"I think I'd like your life, or at least your job," she said, thinking how wonderful it'd be to spend whole days with Bo and the other horses.

Alex opened one eye. "No, you wouldn't." He spoke a little crisply, though it might have been the accent.

"Sure I would. How many horses do you have to look after?"

"It's not really about them, it's the rest of it…" Alex rolled on his side and propped his head on his elbow. He studied her face until her cheeks grew hot. "Why do you ask? I mean, do you wish you could change your life?"

Sass's mouth opened and shut, and no sound come out. All she could hear was the water in the creek.

"Sorry … random question, don't answer that." He sat up, spooking Bo, who'd been dozing behind them like an elderly aunt.

"No, no, it wasn't," Sass answered, "and the answer's — *yes*. Maybe more than you know."

Alex didn't reply and stood up. Offering her a hand, he pulled her up too, the space of a heartbeat between them.

"So why don't you change it?" he asked, more curious than confrontational.

"None of it's really in my control."

She waited for him to say something about making her own destiny, but instead a look of understanding came into his eyes. "Yeah, I know how that feels."

"You're not the impulsive type either, then?"

He raised an eyebrow. "I didn't say that. I never get the chance."

There was a faintly awkward pause.

"So, come on, then. Truth or Dare?" Sass burst out in the thrumming silence.

"Dare?" he replied, tilting his head in a question.

"I dare you to take me riding again. I want to gallop like you did across the sand."

Sass looked in his face. Had she gone too far? Was today a one-off, nothing more? How could she even assume that he'd want to spend any more time with her?

Seconds ticked by. "When?" he said finally.

"How about the end of the week?"

Alex whistled through his teeth. "Come on, that's a dare for you, not me. What if you fall off?" Doubt creased his forehead.

"Answer my question!"

"Okay," he said slowly, "you're on, but you'll need tons more lessons."

Sass swallowed a teeny-tiny urge to squeal because words weren't enough to express how she felt, which was everything good rolled into one.

"How about tomorrow?" he continued. "You're going to have to work hard if you want to gallop that soon." A gruffness had crept into his voice. He was taking it all very seriously and expected the same of her.

Sass managed a nod because her tongue had gone the way of her squeal. As she turned to leave, he reached out and caught her elbow, his fingers touching the soft crease in her arm. They slid to the bones of her wrist.

"Same time tomorrow, then? Don't be late…"

In the drowsy heat of the afternoon, the long grass trembled in the breeze. And a million winged things started clapping.

10

THE VISITOR

Sass skipped home, or at least, her heart did the skipping; her head was spaghetti. Was it the prospect of riding again … or seeing Alex? No. It had to be the riding. She knew better than to fall for the first boy who looked her way. She threw open the back door so hard that yellow paint flakes flew off like sunrays in a little kid's drawing.

"Anyone home?"

Sass kicked off her shoes and dumped her bag, looking around the tiny cottage built for fishermen, now home to artists, with its bulging chalk walls cluttered with so many paintings that the sea was inside and out.

Harry came out of his downstairs cupboard and jumped up at her, and Sass was still making a fuss of him when Jessie walked out of the kitchen.

"Hi, Sass."

"Jessie, you're back!"

"Yeah. Couldn't stay away." She made a rueful face. "Cup of tea?"

"Yes, please. Milk and two sugars."

Tea with its magical healing powers. Sass sipped it slowly so she didn't burn her mouth. Since coming to this country, she'd drunk more tea than ever before. She'd never be a convert, but it worked, and not just for her. Jessie was back, and whatever fight she and David had going on seemed to have sorted itself out. And Sass felt … happy about that. The accident hadn't just turned her life upside down. Besides, Jessie cast a warmth that was impossible to resist. She was look-at-me-beautiful without even trying. Sass glanced down at herself. She pulled off her hairband and shook out her hair. She was like that girl raised by wolves. She was the original Wolf Girl. What must Alex think of her?

When David got back that evening, they all walked up the road to meet the fish-and-chip van. Sitting on the sea wall side by side, they unwrapped their oily newspaper parcels and tucked in. Sass was used to takeout, but not like this: fish in crispy batter dipped in ketchup with hot, thick fries, fresher than a sea breeze.

In the distance, two triangles of sail raced across the horizon, and her world tilted too. Was it possible to feel sad and happy? Losing Mom, moving on, finding Bo and then meeting Alex seemed as bittersweet and totally unexpected as … salted caramel. Maybe this was how life would be now?

Things that shouldn't go together just did, like peanut butter and jelly, which she'd always be true to, however good the fish and chips.

Alex had been lugging straw bales down for the horses. Rubbing the sweat from his face, he strolled through the pale stone archway from the yard. As he rounded the corner, his heart stopped. His father's Aston Martin stood parked at the front of the house: the driver's door open, a gash of red leather against gleaming silver paintwork. He almost backtracked, then changed his mind with a furious swipe at a rosebush, snagging his hand on its thorns. Blood splattered on his breeches as he took the front steps two at a time.

His father stood with his back to him in the faded silk curtained drawing-room, where a solitary bluebottle head-butted the French windows.

"There's no point to you being here," Alex said, managing to keep his cool for about a second. "I won't go back, you can't make me."

In the mirror above the marble fireplace, he caught his old man's gaze: still proud to see his son despite the lousy welcome.

"I've nothing to say to you," Alex continued.

"Then there's no need for you to raise your voice." His father's comment as he turned to face him at last.

Alex shut up, stunned into silence by his own confusion. He gripped the back of a wing chair for support, the old leather creaking. They hadn't spoken since the evening before the Summer Ball, when his father's call had come too late, the journalist's words already ringing in his ears.

Was his mother heartbroken at their break-up? Alex didn't know, but she was the one betrayed first, and that had to count for something, didn't it? Everyone loved her, except Father, it seemed. His mother had visited him at school. Hinted at the coming news, maybe, while she charmed them all. She'd told him she was going away for a few weeks and not to worry, that she'd call, which she had, last night. Probably prodded by Grandma. Said she was "so up and down" by way of explanation.

"If you won't take my calls, then what am I supposed to do? You're my son." His father was speaking. He hardly ever raised his voice because he didn't need to.

"Not something I'm likely to forget."

His father's self-control snapped and frustration spilled out. "For god's sake, sit down. I'm here now."

Alex looked straight into his eyes. Not many people did that, and he felt a brief rush of triumph.

"I don't want to. It's all a mess, so just go. Leave me alone to figure it out like you usually do!"

And he left his father standing there. Alex got as far as the old scullery, where he slumped behind the door and kicked it shut. Who did his father think he was, just turning up?

Alone in the stuffy heat of the drawing-room, the heir to the throne thought rather differently.

11

CRESSIDA SLATER

Cressida Slater, gossip columnist for the Daily Sun, yawned behind her hand and slouched in her Jimmy Choos. She adjusted her sunglasses and squinted at the polo ponies galloping up the field. His Royal Highness was taking the game very seriously. He'd arrived late and was making up for it. She watched the red-faced older man furiously trying to ride off his rival, a smooth Argentine, who it was rumoured had dazzled his wife, Princess Seraphina, since their split. The Princess was the most glamorous woman on the planet. It didn't look like a royal reconciliation was likely any time soon.

Cressida was pleased with her latest scoop: delivering the news of the official separation to the son. It hadn't been easy. She'd had to cycle a mile up a boggy towpath, skulk about in bushes and then screech across a river. Had totally sunk the poor boy, though. She allowed herself a slight smirk. The look on his face? Priceless. Literally. The photos had sold worldwide. Alexander was growing up fast and had girls in a twitter all over the world. Not that he enjoyed the attention. Quite the opposite, like his father. But the delightful thing was that the moodier he got, the more interesting the young prince became.

And now she had new information from a reliable source, the boy's disgruntled ex-copper, always an advantage. After she'd delivered the news, there had been a school ball and some gossip involving an heiress called Plum that had led the boy to bunk off to his grandmother's in Cornwall. His bodyguard had got the boot, et voilà, she had the beginnings of her next story.

The trouble with scoops was that one was never enough. You needed dollops of the mush and the Daily Sun wanted more. "That boy," her editor had said over a fag out the back by the Thames, "is the future. I want it all. How he's doing, who he's snogging, the name of his pet hamster. The lot. Readers are tired of his parents, a squabbling middle-aged couple, and you — Cressida —" A puff of blue smoke. "Are the one to make it happen!"

12

PRACTICE MAKES PERFECT

Since the moment Alex said: "same time tomorrow", the words had been swimming in Sass's head like shiny silver fish. She tried to walk calmly to the meadow but couldn't keep herself from skipping, and it wasn't long before Bo was looking up at her as if to say, "Back so soon?", her black eyes blinking in the dappled sunshine by the creek. Each time, it seemed, the walk got a little shorter and the wall a little lower. Sass had arrived first and it was Alex's turn to be late. For ten minutes or so, she sat on the step to the trailer. The first time she'd been there, she hadn't been welcome, and it felt odd even now to be sitting outside.

Inside the narrow door swinging on its hinges, she could see Bo's halter hanging on a peg, next to a beat-up cream sweater with a trailing sleeve that she guessed was Alex's. She reached up and touched the hand-knitted wool. Unmistakably English, it had a deep "V" neck and stripy trim.

One minute, it was hanging there, and the next it had dropped into her lap. Sass bunched it up and went to put it back, and it was then that she noticed what was behind it.

The black bridle matched Bo's halter, with its beautiful stitching, padded leather and brass buckles. She touched it and the metal bit that went in the horse's mouth clinked slightly. Sass looked across the meadow. "Come on, Alex!" she whispered. Surely he hadn't forgotten? Maybe he couldn't get away? He did have a job, after all. She stilled the small anxiety that he'd got in trouble after last time, or worse, he'd changed his mind.

Sass took the bridle and went outside to wait; she'd need it for when he came. She held it up next to Bo, but the mare flicked her tail and put her head down to eat. If she could figure it out, she could show Alex that she wasn't just some useless city girl. Besides, a bridle looked a lot like a halter, and Alex had showed her how that went. Sass put the reins over Bo's neck so she had something to hang on to. She could see how it worked, it was just a question of getting the mare to lift her head...

"Open wide — Ew!"

Bo's teeth were huge. With a hand on the horse's nose, Sass held the metal bit in her palm with a mint from her pocket. Wet lips, green with drool, made a lunge for it. Luckily, Bo knew exactly how the bridle should go and Sass managed to slip the whole thing on. It was a little lopsided and she had no idea what to do with all the straps, so she just did them up loose.

"Hey!" She stood back. "Good job."

She kissed Bo's minty nose: they were ready. All she needed now was her instructor. Where was he? Sass led Bo over to the hay bale that propped up the trailer. She could get on and wait, couldn't she? Having come this far, Alex might be pleased that she'd got ahead.

Even from on top of the haystack there was a gulf between her and the horse. She took a breath and counted. "One, two, three — oomf!" Sass threw herself on just as Bo began to wander down to the creek. Somehow Sass got her leg over and wriggled up Bo's spine, the mare's back muscles wobbling like Jell-O on a plate. No wonder they invented the bicycle. Sitting there, she remembered her lesson with Alex. That time, she hadn't steered because he'd been leading her, but now, holding the reins, she felt good doing it for herself.

"Okay, girl. Come on."

She prodded the mare's sides with her heels, alarmed when it worked and Bo plunged forward.

"Okay, easy on the gas." She straightened up and as she adjusted her weight, she was surprised when the horse slowed down again. What should she do now? Maybe once around the meadow?

At first, Sass was happy with Bo wandering along stopping to snatch at the long grass like it was her own personal snack tour, but it was a little aimless. More initiative was needed. Next time Bo put her head down, Sass gave her a little kick and flapped the reins. Startled, the mare flung up her head and broke into a ragged, bone-rattling trot.

"Okay, all right. I'll ask nicer next time." Sass didn't feel scared; the opposite was true. Sure, she was sitting on a living, breathing, hairy trampoline, but it was kind of wonderful. She practised it again. Gentler this time. A squeeze and a click with her tongue like she'd seen. Walk, trot. Walk, trot. Until they got it. The last time, Bo broke into a lope. It only lasted a few rocking-horse strides, but Sass felt that in that moment she was airborne. Cloud nine slid across the sky. She was staying on board forever.

What next? She couldn't just go around and around. She'd follow the creek path downstream and meet Alex coming the other way. Anyway, Bo seemed to know where she was heading, so Sass let her, and they puttered along the damp springy grass next to where the water shimmered with dragonflies. At the end of the meadow, they came to a gate half hanging off its hinges.

Maybe she should have turned around and gone back, but instead Sass dragged it open. She went through and was just bending to shut it again when a fat ginger cat streaked out from underneath with a yowl. Bo shied sideways and Sass tumbled off. A clumsy fall that landed her with a splat in the churned-up gateway on the other side. By the time she looked up, Bo had hightailed it over the hill. Sass's solo adventure had come to a messy end.

13

NOT THE WILD WEST

Alex had finished mucking out. He dumped the last loaded wheelbarrow, shrugging off more than a slight feeling of emptiness. His father had gone, had a charity polo match to play. Alex hadn't waited to see him off; there wasn't much point, since they still weren't speaking.

His thoughts turned to Sass. He pictured her pulling faces at the cows and felt slightly better. She really didn't seem to know who he was, and he still couldn't believe it was true. Where had she been all his life? He laughed. An unreal sound. If he hadn't been so down, he might have found it funny. Yesterday, when she burst out with Truth or Dare, the dare had been a no-brainer. Why did she want to gallop before she could walk? He'd seen tell-tale shadows under her eyes. Did she have parent hassle too? Or was she just a speed freak like him? Fear made things clearer like cold water on skin. He stretched his back. There was something different about her. She wasn't the same as other girls he could think of. Plum Benoist slid uninvited into his mind.

He'd first met Plum down at the school boathouse a few months ago. He and the rest of the First VIII had been training for the National Schools' Regatta. He loved the freedom of the river, even in winter when it was freezing and all they saw as they swept along were ducks and the occasional swan. After a two-mile run that morning, they'd warmed up and were ready to row, conscious of a group of schoolgirls pointing on the opposite bank.

"Looking good, Your Highness," Gully had joked as they collected their boat and carried it down to the river. Gully sat in the bow, all six-foot-five of him, like a Viking warrior. Loved all female attention. As stroke, Alex sat in the stern, setting the rhythm and pace.

"Yeah, waggle your bum for the cameras. You know that's what they're here for." His crewmate Ollie showed him how to do it as they bent to pick up eight painted oars from the ground, the blades a flash of gold in the morning sun.

"Who's standing in for Will, then?" Alex asked, since their cox was off.

"It's a girl. . ." Ollie drawled.

"Yeah, right." Alex had added to the banter. It seemed easiest.

"No, really! Don't look now, here she comes."

Alex had turned, of course . . . and put his foot in the fat hole that was his mouth.

With a swish of platinum blonde hair, Plum had walked towards them in skintight purple Lycra.

"Now you know how she got her name," Ollie whispered evilly. But it was her eyes that Alex noticed first. Beautiful like a cat's and fixed firmly on him.

Alex shook his head and parked the wheelbarrow, whistling for Susan, chuffed when the old Labrador shambled after him towards the park that in turn led to the fields beyond. He'd be late meeting Sass, but still when the old dog lagged behind, he slowed down too and took in his surroundings. High up in a sky so white that it dazzled, a kestrel hovered as if Trist were on her watch today. The bird floated on the air, awesome and free, while down in the shadow of the oaks, Alex could see the old estate was showing her age. The post-and-rail fencing around the lower paddocks was warped and flaking. Twigs and leaves filled the empty water troughs, while ragwort, cow parsley and nettles choked the field gates. His inheritance. And the rest. Was it possible to have too much? He just wanted to be left to live here instead of dealing with the chaos that followed his parents. He knew he had responsibilities, but didn't he have a right to a life of his own?

Sass couldn't see Bo. She staggered to her feet in the puddle, losing one shoe, then the other, only to slither in the sludge and plonk down again. Her hands and bum were covered in it. Then she made the mistake of pushing her hair out of her face, and a fat glob of ooze dribbled down her cheek. Glaring up at the sun, she shaded her eyes across an empty hillside. Oh god, where had Bo galloped off to? Sass made a desperate wish.

A wet-nosed panting and a raspy tongue wasn't what she had in mind. She squinted: a chocolate-brown Labrador with meaty breath had just licked her knee, and standing behind the dog was Alex holding Bo. Her heart leapt.

"Lost something?" He grinned.

"You found her. Thank you! I'm so sorry. A stupid cat ran out and I fell off."

"So I see. Did you have to pick a puddle?"

"I didn't get to choose."

"You could have waited for me before getting on?"

"I know, I know, please don't be mad, but you were late and I couldn't..."

"I should've guessed."

He helped her up and Sass squashed against him with a slight squelch. He held Bo steady while she got back on using the wonky gate, reins bunched in one hand.

"I'm sorry that I didn't wait. I should have."

Alex didn't say anything, but leaned over instead to correct her hands.

"This is England, Sass, not the Wild West — like this, with your thumbs on top. And stretch your legs down and move your ankles about."

Sass looked down at her filthy shoes turned out Charlie-Chaplin style against Bo's warm sides. She needed riding boots.

She needed dry pants, underwear too, but she was forgiven.

"How does that feel?"

"Better, thanks."

"Riding bareback is good for your seat."

"My what?" Sass asked.

"Your b ... balance," he said quickly. "You've got to get your position right."

"It wasn't Bo's fault that I fell off." Sass leaned forward to stroke the horse's neck.

"I guessed that. Did you know, real riders never blame their horses?"

"You think I could be?"

"What? A rider. Course, why not?"

"We've trotted already." She pulled herself taller, her confidence returning.

"Show me, then. Bet you didn't go rising?"

"Go what?"

"When Bo starts trotting, hold on to her mane and try to feel the rhythm of her movement. Her legs will move in diagonal pairs and all you've got to do is go with it. Up, down. Up, down. Try not to bounce about too much. I should warn you, though..." He grinned. "It's almost impossible without a saddle and stirrups."

"But if it's impossible —" she began.

"Give it a try," he said firmly. He clicked with his tongue and Bo set off down the creek path with Alex's hand on Sass's ankle to keep it in place.

14

WHITE LIES

They didn't get as far as the sea, but by the time they stopped, both were hot and breathless. Alex watched Sass lead Bo down to the creek to drink.

"It's annoying, you're a natural-born rider, you know?" He wiped his face on his arm.

"Yeah. I'll be giving you lessons soon." Her eyes danced slightly as she took him in, her fingers twisted in Bo's mane.

"Bo's a good teacher," he carried on, feeling bolder. "She taught me too."

"Did she? I knew she was important to you."

Alex didn't answer at first, although the way she was with Bo made him want to trust her, to tell her things. Things nobody knew.

"It was after she had Dancer. I was ten and ready to move up to horses."

"Were you hanging out at the stables or something?"

Alex swallowed. He'd gone too far and yet not far enough. It would be so good to have someone to talk to, share stuff with.

Her face held his gaze, but he knew that the moment he set the record straight, everything would change. Who he was shaped his life. Why would a girl with half a brain want to be tangled up with him?

"Yes — sort of. Just a kid, you know, helping out in the holidays."

"But you're Welsh, right, not Cornish? Not from around here?"

He paused. His heart hammered hard. "What makes you say that?" She'd blindsided him again.

Sass read his face with a slight frown. "I don't know — you're a Wales fan, then? At cricket, or soccer or whatever you Brits play. I just thought that maybe you were because the sweatshirt you're wearing has 'WALES' on the back."

"What — this?" He twisted around, tugging at his favourite rowing shirt. "Can't remember where I got this. School, maybe."

"Oh — okay," she said, as if she believed him, when Alex knew she couldn't because he was confused enough himself. He cast around for the nearest something to distract her, anything but talking about himself any more. His eyes landed on the knotted green hedge that had bordered the creek for as long as he could remember. A shelter for sheep and horses, but also foxes, badgers, hedgehogs and deer. Once he'd even seen an otter scoot to the water's edge.

He took Sass by the hand. She was so close, he could smell her damp skin.

Was he lying? He was showing her everything he loved best.

Wasn't that better than the truth?

When Alex took her hand, Sass felt her pulse quicken. She thought he might kiss her, but instead he crouched down, pulling her with him as he pointed to something near the ground. Sass knelt and looked. Nestling between mossy stones and bright green leaves was a cluster of strawberries. Wild ones. Tiny, dimpled fruit like rubies in a velvet glove. He let go of her hand to pick one, hesitant as he held it to her lips. A sharp burst of juice touched her tongue and trickled stickily down her chin.

He picked a whole handful and they sat down on the grass. "So tell me what Brooklyn is like. That's where you're from, right?" Sass startled, shocked to hear her home named out loud.

Shocked that he even remembered. A lump rose in her throat.

When would she walk again down that dirty, honking street where she'd spent her whole life? A life that was over. Yesterday was gone and today ... today she was here in this Cornish place, where even the smallest berry was suddenly strangely precious, a treasure she hadn't even known existed before. It was all so perfectly — confusing.

" — and what do you get up to there?"

"What do I do?" Sass stalled. She scrunched her toes in her canvas shoes. "Y'know..." She shrugged, keeping it light and fake. "School, hanging out with friends, shopping, the usual things." She pushed the ache away. It was too soon to tell him. "And you?" she asked, desperate to switch the subject.

"Same. Sort of. Hate school, except PE and history; they're okay. Loathe Latin."

"Me too." She agreed. School was a safe, neutral subject, like saying her favourite colour was beige, when it wasn't, it was red.

He looked at her again. He didn't believe her, she could tell.

Sass had never done Latin in her life. What sort of school still taught it? Not one that she knew of.

Alex carried on. "The horses, of course, they come with my job. And the dog."

"The dog comes with your job?"

He scowled.

"She's a working dog. She retrieves things..." He frowned slightly and reached down to fiddle with Susan's collar. "So are you still up for the dare?"

"I am, if you are?" Sass kept her voice airy. Happy-go-unlucky. "But if I'm going to die galloping, I'd like to know your full name. I'm Sass. Short for Saskia Emerson."

He stepped forward. "I'm Alex. Alexander..." He struggled with his words before scrabbling in his pocket. "I forgot —I brought you this."

"What is it?"

77

"It's a key. Don't they have those in the States?"

"I mean, what lock does it fit?" She turned it over in her hand like it was some relic.

"It's so you don't have to keep climbing the wall."

"You figured out my secret way in, huh? You won't get in trouble, letting me have this, will you? I wouldn't want you to lose your job."

Eyes the colour of burnt sugar met hers and the last part of her melted.

"Lose my job?" he said slowly. "Don't worry — there's no chance of that."

And they went their separate ways, with only a mile of white lies between them.

15

THE BEE'S KNEES

Plum Benoist was cross. She'd finished doing her nails, which was hard if you were angry. She waggled them dry with a small scowl. She'd get them re-done at the nail bar tomorrow. Her hair, newly highlighted, was smoothed in place and held back by a band that pulled at her skin with a satisfying sting. She got up and put the Topshop nail polish back in its place; it slotted between 'Prim and Proper' and 'Bee's Knees'.

So boring at home. Thank god she had the gym. Pilates, or spinning, perhaps both. She stood in front of the double doors of her mirrored wardrobe. Marta, the horse-faced family housekeeper, was singing as she vacuumed the house in the background. God, it was a dump. The thing about minimalist – open plan, all white, and glass – that her "interior designer" and stepmother, Brooke, should have known, was that it only worked if everything was spotless. Perhaps Brooke had banked on the girls not being there, having Daddy all to herself? That was never going to happen, like ever.

She heard her eldest sister Cerise come in the front door and drop her shopping. Wasn't there a limit on her credit card? If not, that wasn't fair either. Cee-ce would step out of her shoes in the hallway and just leave her bags as if bored already.

Plum was aware that at sixteen, she was unusual in being quite so obsessive, but detail was important. She was a girl with ambition, stuck with a ridiculous name. She'd change it one day. Named after a fruit, so . . . icky. She fluttered her hands as if a wasp were buzzing near. So yawningly dull waiting for nail polish to dry.

If Cee-ce was on her own, then where was Bosie? Had Framboise even got up yet? Her eldest sister was nocturnal. She'd be out again clubbing tonight. Her dress sense was about as subtle as a bash to the head. She was dating a footballer: Chelsea or Fulham, perhaps one of each.

With a small sigh, Plum thought back to the Summer Ball, the highlight of her school term. She was good at most things, especially the things that mattered. And what mattered most was being the best. A* at everything and nothing less would do. Take Alex. It wasn't that she liked him, or rather, she didn't like-*like* him, but it was important for her to know that she had a chance with him. Daddy had taught her to be a winner, when he remembered who she was. His youngest daughter stabbed at a red pinch mark on the inside of her wrist. His Sugar Plum. Right now, she was losing.

Her phone tinkled: silver calfskin, studded with Swarovski crystals. Text message. Plum sighed, glancing down at the screen because it wasn't Alex; it was her BFF, Millie, bored in Tuscany.

Hi babes, how's it going? Found this! Soz.
Love ya :)

Plum opened the accompanying image. Blinking back at her was Alex, her Royal Disappointment. She opened the image to its max. He appeared to be flinching from her kiss at the Ball. *No!* That hadn't been right; she'd have known. He hadn't liked the camera flashes in his face afterwards, that's all. She squeezed the image down like a spot needing attention. It stung that he'd not called, or even replied to her texts. She'd looked amazing in that last selfie. No boy had ever ignored her. A failure? No, a setback. Like Boxercise, you just had to keep dancing and punching low. Maybe he needed a nudge? Bosie knew someone on the *Daily Sun*. Some nosy journalist called Cressida Slater. Perhaps she should call her, just for a chat? They could help each other. A photo for a favour. Plum didn't expect to find fame all by herself.

16

RETAIL THERAPY

Sass got back to the cottage aching, grass-stained, caked in mud, sunburned, sticky, and not a little sweaty. Even her uncle had looked up from the sketch he was working on and raised an eyebrow, while Harry simply stuck his nose in like she was the smelliest, best girl in the world.

"What have you been up to?" David asked. Sass felt herself go pink. "I slipped and fell..."

And it was then that Jessie, who had been looking at her sideways, jumped in to save her.

"I'm going shopping, want to come?"

"Shopping?" Sass repeated. Had Jessie noticed that she needed new clothes, or was she just plain psychic? Not that she had much money. She frowned. If any — did she? She hadn't really thought about all that. Maybe Uncle David understood because he reached in his back pocket and, with a glance at Jessie, pulled out some folded notes from his wallet.

"Get yourself something nice," he said gruffly.

Soon they were on their way to Bloomingdale's – okay, maybe not, but the nearest thing – in the Land Rover, which creaked and groaned and bounced over every pothole, and hill.

"Don't worry — we should get there." Jessie crunched the gears and risked a glance across at Sass. "You should have said if you needed things."

"I didn't want to ask. You guys have done so much for me already."

"Please, you mustn't worry about that. David's not one for saying much, but I know how much he wants it to work out between you."

"He does?"

"Yes!" Jessie swung the car to the side and tugged the handbrake on. "And I do too. It was a change, of course, having you here, and I can't imagine how hard it's been for you, but . . ," She squeezed Sass's hand. "You're with us now. You're part of our life."

Sass didn't know how to reply. She squeezed Jessie's hand hard back.

"So what do you need?"

"Almost everything. I packed the wrong stuff. I need boots — I think."

"Boots! It's summer." Jessie stuck her arm out of the window to signal that she was pulling out again.

"I know — Maybe some new jeans too?"

"Yes, I saw what happened to your old ones." Jessie

risked a glance at her and smiled. "We could also pop into the hairdresser's for a trim, if you wanted."

Sass brought her hand up to her ponytail. "I don't think I could."

"Why not? I mean, it's lovely, but you could add some layers, or shape."

Sass paused, imagining her hair gone. "I don't know — Mom, she likes — liked, it longer."

"I know, but my love, you get to decide now."

"I suppose I do." Her chin wobbled.

"Well, then. It's your choice. I know a good salon that might just be able to fit you in."

"This afternoon?" Sass looked out at the blur of green rushing past the window.

"Yes. Shall I give them a ring?"

"Okay, well — why not! It's just hair, right? It'll grow."
"Good! First, I want to take you to my favourite shop. It's vintage, mind. Do you like vintage? Not everyone does."

"I love vintage."

"Then we're going to have fun!"

The cathedral town of Truro was stuffed with people, most of them tourists. As there was nowhere to park, Jessie had to point the way to the shop, "Retro-ve", while she drove off to find a space. Worst case, they'd meet at the salon where Jessie had begged her an appointment. Jessie's only request was that Sass find something to wear to the wedding of her and David's friends on Saturday. Sass, it seemed, was tagging along too. Not that Jessie had put it that way.

Sass headed down a crooked side street. The shop front had a retro neon sign outside that said "ENJOY!". She pushed the door open, and inside looked exactly how she imagined the backstage dressing room of a really old theatre, the room soft-lit by light bulbs framing long, dusty mirrors. An old jukebox pumped out some sort of jazzy hip hop, and in the corner a purple velvet couch lounged beside racks and racks of clothes that smelled of exotic and slightly stale perfume. The shop assistant came over — a frightening resemblance to Marilyn Monroe in biker boots and skin-tight gold lamé. Better than being styled by wolves, Sass thought.

"Can I help you?" Marilyn asked in a low voice and an accent Sass hadn't heard before in Cornwall. Maybe Irish or Scottish? After assessing Sass with a kohl-black eye, Marilyn went off and found her an armful of things that she hung in a small fitting-room, her bracelets jangling as she closed the curtain.

"Just shout if you need anything." Her voice had a definite lilt that sang out across the shop floor. Was she Welsh? Sass thought of Alex's sweatshirt. She couldn't help it. On the back, it had definitely said "WALES", the letters embroidered in white on black. On his chest had been a smaller crest with a pair of crossed ... paddles? That had to tell her something about him. Maybe his school was there, or he once kayaked for a Welsh school team?

Sass picked out a tea dress from the 1930s. It said so in a hand-written swirl on the label hanging from its padded hanger. She swooshed the dress around her in the mirror and imagined it on a girl called Daphne drinking Lapsang Souchong tea from a china cup. She touched the fabric. It was made of air: an ivory silk printed with tiny birds and entwined with flowers that had faded in places. She slipped it on; light as dust, the short sleeves gathered at the cuff, and the high waistband was edged in a delicate lace. Daphne wasn't as tall as she was, so the waist was higher and the hem a lot shorter. Sass's knees stuck out, brown from the sun and, she wet her thumb and rubbed at them, still dirty. She shrugged her hips left and right, and the fabric lifted and spun. It was beautiful. She could float out of the shop and over the sea like the paper lantern David had lit the first night that she came.

While the dress was being wrapped in silver tissue, Sass chose a few other things. In five minutes, the pile by the till had grown to a pair of blue skinny jeans from like way back in the 1980s; a floral kimono; a pair of cropped dungarees; a tan shoulder bag; and a pair of Chelsea boots that secretly Sass knew she could ride in. She glanced up at the clock. Still no Jessie; where was she?

Sass found her own way to the hair salon. It was the sort of place where even the hairdryers were hushed. Her hairstylist, Giacomo, was dressed in head-to-toe black like an Italian-Cornish samurai with scissors. He had stubble and a scowly smile, and a voice that made her feel embarrassed. He shampooed her at the basin with firm hands, leaning in to growl: "*L'acqua troppo calda?*" Sass got the word for *hot* and hoped it didn't look weird if she closed her eyes.

At the mirror, Giacomo towelled her hair and teased her tangles with his fingers until he'd tamed it around her shoulders. Then, assuming what she wanted was what he wanted to do, he pressed her head forward, and with one hand on her neck and the other on what looked like a cut-throat razor, he began snipping and zipping as he layered her hair. Occasionally he'd bend forward and blow the hair from her neck, and Sass watched it curl to the ground, trying to imagine what Alex would say when he saw her.

Would he tease her? Would he notice her at all? She was telling herself off for even thinking of him when a face in the mirror made her heart stop.

The woman opposite had a magazine open, its front cover visible in the glass. Ignoring Giacomo's restraining hand, Sass edged forward to the front of her seat. A boy who looked a lot like Alex glowered back, although the headline couldn't possibly be true. She stared again with a dawning recognition, the colour draining from her cheeks.

PRINCE ALEXANDER, THE FACE OF THE FUTURE.

It couldn't be? And yet it was. Unless the Alex she knew was some sort of double? A prince. No way. That was totally nuts. She stood up, pulling at the silky, black gown, now tight at her throat.

"*Cosa stai facendo, bella?*"

With trembling hands, Sass stepped over to the woman. She had to check. "Excuse me, but please — may I see your magazine?"

"But I'm reading it!" the woman spluttered, the towel on her head unravelling.

"I'm sorry, but I just want to — I need to take a look." The woman must have seen her face because she sucked her teeth and handed it over.

It was him.

The unmistakable, guarded dark eyes. Only better looking and kind of photo-smoothed out. An expertly lit shadow ran down his jaw. Sass gripped the picture so hard that the centre section of the magazine came away and fell to the floor, leaving her clutching the empty cover. With the full disapproval of a salon of shocked eyes, her hair still dripping down her back, Sass gathered it up and ran out of the door. The wind would blow-dry her hair, but nothing, nothing, could hush the rush of blood in her ears.

In her bedroom at home, Plum pored over the full article on her iPad mini. Cressida had used one of the pictures taken a few months back by Mario Testosterone, or whatever his name was, to mark Alex's sixteenth birthday. It was after the photos came out that the girls at school began rushing down to the riverbank whenever he was rowing. She'd put a stop to that. As head girl, she got first dibs. The uglies could get in line. She read the accompanying article. It didn't say much about her, and no picture, but it was just about enough. A perfect mention like a teeny-tiny hint. A frisson ran though her like a sugar rush.

The prince is currently linked to Plum Benoist, the beautiful and talented youngest daughter of fruit and vegetable billionaire Vincent Benoist.

Daddy would be pleased. It wasn't often that she got in the news. Usually it was her father's business takeovers, her stepmother's interiors, or snaps of Cee-ce and Bosie coming out of restaurants pretending to hide their faces. She stroked the words, pausing over the last line of the article.

The prince is spending the summer at Trist, the ancestral home of his maternal grandmother, the Countess of Tremayne, in Cornwall, where he awaits official confirmation of the divorce of his parents.

Poor Alex; he really needed her with him. She'd said as much to Cressida, who had absolutely agreed. Plum could see the next photo shoot already: the one with her in it. They'd have puppies, golden ones, scampering around. Alex liked dogs. She didn't especially, but wouldn't mind this once. They'd have a picnic laid out on a huge tartan rug, nothing messy so her dress didn't get marked. Her hair would blow about ... unless she wore a hat? One of those fantastic floppy ones that cost loads but looked hippie chic. Hmm ... it might drown her, or get in the way if he ever kissed her properly. Plum glanced down at her phone and pursed her lips. She'd switched it to silent to avoid further humiliation, which wasn't a word she understood. Once Alex saw this article, he'd remember why he needed her. She could shelter him from the attention that he so detested because she didn't mind it at all. She was born to shine in the limelight, not be stuck in the shadow of her sisters. She was like . . . Cinderella. Okay, she'd dozens of shoes, but she also had the stepmother, the sisters, the dozy prince and now she wanted that glass slipper, more than a Versace handbag in the Harrods Summer Sale.

17

ANY GIRL'S DREAM

Outside the salon, Sass bent forward with her hands on her knees. Breathe, Sass, breathe! So many thoughts raced in her head, hiding what had to be a simple explanation. He wasn't a prince. Was he, was he, was he? The words went fuzzy. She lifted her head and saw that Giacomo and the salon manager had loomed up in front of her.

Thankfully, so had Jessie.

"Sass! What's happened?" She rushed up. "Why are you standing out here with your hair all wet?"

Over the hubbub of the street, Sass heard the stilted English of Giacomo's answer. Her eyes slid from their faces. "I — I had a bad moment, that's all." She scrunched the magazine behind her back, as if hiding it from sight meant it had gone away, like a game of peekaboo with herself. Except she wasn't a baby; she was all grown up.

Somehow Jessie persuaded the others back inside while Sass watched through the glass as she clearly explained about

Mom — because Giacomo's body language softened and he kissed her on both cheeks, flapping away all payment.

A free haircut *and* a prince. Any girl's dream. So why wasn't she feeling it?

Because Alex had taken her for a fool.

Deep down, she knew it was him on the front of that magazine. She even recognised his face now. The only plausible reason she hadn't before was because no girl met a prince in the middle of a field. Definitely not a girl with bad hair, a long way from Brooklyn. A new, dumber version of herself, seen through Alex's eyes, was forming in her head, as anger replaced amazement. She was mad at herself, but even madder at him.

How could he not have told her? Was she supposed to have guessed? Did he think she knew? Oh god! She was the one who'd trespassed, climbed a wall and down a cliff to spy on him; who'd messed with his stuff; ridden his horse in cutoff shorts and dared him to take her galloping. Her shoulders slumped, her hair sopping wet. Did he think she was desperate, or just some airhead from the States that it'd be fun to fool around with for a summer? That American girls were easy and stupid...

The journey back was horrible; only the rattling of the car filled the silence. The rolled-up magazine was a smoking gun inside the shopping bag by her feet.

"Honestly, Sass, it looks lovely," Jessie kept repeating. Like this was about hair.

That night, Alex sat on the roof at Trist listening to the silence, his feet dangling and the slate solid at his back. Whenever it was hot and he couldn't sleep, he'd climb out of his attic bedroom onto the narrow ledge that ran along the length of the house like a piecrust. It helped him to think. He could walk right around and balance on the brink. He wasn't the first. During the Second World War, the Air Force had stayed here, most of them young officers not much older than he was. He'd found their names and dates scratched on the wall behind him. He wondered how many of them had come back from the war.

Tonight there were no stars in the sky, just a half moon and the winking lights of a passenger plane flying overhead towards London. It reminded him of her. Sass had come three thousand miles across the Atlantic and stumbled into his world. He still didn't know that much about her; she was always so vague about herself and he didn't like to push it because it could only lead back to him. He'd tell her the truth when he was sure that she liked him, not just some idiot she'd read about.

He knew that she came from Brooklyn, New York, and was staying with her uncle in the village. Sass had told him a bit about her life. The usual stuff that he couldn't do. One day maybe he'd get to go where he wanted, hang out with friends too. Maybe he'd find it easier with girls. But which girl? Sass seemed to get him, but would she see past who he was? Plum saw what she wanted.

Alex drummed his heels. He hadn't even asked her how long she was staying. It might not be the whole summer and the thought bothered him. He looked down on the world from his eagle's nest. Made out where the slope of the South Lawn, fussed over every day by old Roberts, gave up to a crooked slash of black, where the creek, hidden from sight, threaded its way down from the ridge that curved around the estate, past the meadow, to the sea. On a bright day, if he scrambled up the roof and leaned right over the weathervane, he could see where the stream ended, fingers of water in an open palm reaching across pale shingle and sand.

He had a plan for the dare and he looked forward to seeing her face. If they galloped across that line of sand, then he'd tell her — he'd dare her to go out with him. He picked up a gleaming chip of granite, put his shoulder back, and threw it. It curved through the air like a shooting star. She made him feel stronger. Different. He'd tear up the rule book that said she shouldn't, that she wasn't good enough for him. Not the right sort of girl.

Sleepless in the early hours, Sass crept around Harry, who was rolled in a furry ball, making twitchy sounds while he dreamed. She pulled on her mother's old top and snuck down from the boat-shed to watch the ocean. Every day it changed, its moods as complicated as her own.

"It's a falling tide," said her uncle. She hadn't noticed him skimming pebbles in the darkness. Seemed she hadn't noticed enough.

"That's a good name for it. You're up early?" Having him there felt oddly OK.

"I was worried about you. Jessie said something happened yesterday? You didn't come in and just rushed up to the studio. What was it? I'd like to help if I can."

Sass regarded his steady eyes. Mom's eyes again. And so much welled up inside her that deciding if a boy liked her didn't seem like the hardest thing in the world. Losing Mom was that. Meeting Alex? Well, that was a chance in a million and it had happened to her. Fate could go both ways, couldn't it? Good luck and bad, a double slam. Mom used to say that the most important thing was that she believed in herself, which right now was really hard because how could she, with a hole where her heart was?

"David..." She stumbled a little. "Not long ago, you said I was like my mom. What did you mean?"

A frown crossed her uncle's face. He studied his feet, stubbing his foot against a rock.

"Laura —" he paused, saying her mother's name as if he was out of practice — "was strong; much stronger than me. She was my big sister. She took care of things —"

Sass cut in. "But she never talked about family, or any of this? Or —" she hesitated, putting it on the line — "said anything about you. I don't understand. I mean, why not?"

"I doubt she wanted to. I was out of her life. I don't blame her; there wasn't much she could say, other than I was a stupid, beyond-selfish kid not much older than you when I took off. I hurt her badly when I came here."

He straightened up and looked Sass in the face.

"Just because you don't talk to someone, or the truth is unclear, doesn't mean you don't care, or think about them, or love them any less. Saying it isn't meaning it. It just helps. A lot. And I'm telling you, Sass, that I'm here for you now. Whatever it takes, I'll make up for the rest."

Sass let the words steep like hot tea in a pot. So much was kept in everyone's heads. All the secret-feelings stuff. The stuff that didn't come easily. Maybe Alex had wanted to tell her who he was but couldn't find the right time; too tongue-tied, too awkward, too many animals in the way. It was that, or maybe he didn't care as much as she'd hoped. She shuffled her feet in the shingle. There were so many things she'd go back and tell Mom if she only could.

They stood side by side on the shore, and David reached out and drew her into a rough hug. She leaned against him, the wool of his navy sweater scratchy on her cheek as the tide pulled back to give them space.

18

FORGET IT

It was the day before she was supposed to see Alex again. What should she do, or say? How could she think of anything else right now? Where were the answers? It wasn't like he owed her anything except an explanation — if that. They hadn't even kissed. All they'd had — all she thought they had — was a connection. A thing. Sentences split apart until the words seemed to be bobbing in the sea.

Forgive

    Forget

        Mistake.

    Lies.

        Sense.

Stupidity.

Truth.

Trust.

Used

Liked.

Love.

Lost.

Misunderstood.

He said.

She said.

Yes.

No.

Maybe.

Never.

Ever?

19

A GIRL LIKE HER

It was Friday: fine, bright and clear. Perfect for a gallop. And a dare. Alex dressed quickly in smarter khaki breeches and a rowing top. He never much cared about what he wore, but seeing Sass made him give everything a second glance.

Down on the yard, the radio was on and the horses were stamping for their feeds. Amy peered sleepily from around a tower of buckets.

"Morning, Alex. What are you doing down already?" "Thought I'd give you a hand, as it's Figgy's half day."

"Aw, thank you. That's nice but you really didn't have to." "I know —" he took the buckets from her, — "but I wanted to."

Amy seemed to uncurl and gave him a soft, pleased look that made him wonder, uncomfortably, if she'd misinterpreted his comment.

"I'll do the feeds," he said quickly, "then I'll sort out Dancer."

Head groom Figgy looked up from poulticing a foot. One of the brood mares had trodden on a flint last week. Figgy had worked for Grandma for years, her late father the estate manager back in the day when there'd been a whole string of racehorses in the yard. As schoolgirls, she and Mum had been friends, as opposite as a Shire and a fine Arabian, but while Mum had left, Figgy had stayed. Couldn't leave the animals, Grandma said. Alex knew that if his parents divorced, his mother would never come back. Trist was too weather-bound, too remote and perfect, and all too soon it would probably be gone.

The older woman was glaring at him. No standing on ceremony there; Figgy knew him too well. The thought of her guessing what he was up to made him almost want to bottle it.

"Dancer's had his hay, but you can do the rest. Don't make a mess. And don't distract Amy from her work; she has plenty to be getting on with. I'm off later, remember?"

He'd banked on it.

Figgy straightened up and stretched her back. All the staff were worried about the Trist sale rumours. Father could stop them if he wanted to. He knew what this estate meant to him, his son; the whole village, for that matter. It might be dwarfed by the bigger picture — Alex swallowed hard — but this place, this corner, he wanted to save and not just for himself. Alex took out his penknife and slashed at the baler twine twisted tight around a stack of hay. As the pale sections fell away, he smelled sweet, green meadow grass and clover, and felt calmer. Sass rose late on purpose. She scowled at her reflection and got mad at her hair for sticking out. It had dried wonkily, like the twist of uncertainty in her chest. She was wearing a shirt of Jessie's, the new-old skinny jeans, but not the boots in case they jinxed her; wearing those in the hope of riding was way too much. Last night she'd wanted the dream horses to come and show her what to do. She'd even gone to bed with the painting propped where she could see it.

But they hadn't come.

Feeling more alone than in a long time, Sass touched the brown freckle above her lip in the mirror. It wasn't a freckle, she decided. It was a mole. A big ugly mole that she hated. Pressing her palm to the cold glass, she made up her mind. Forget galloping, but she'd go see Alex and ask him to explain. The thought made her hands shake.

It was mid-afternoon when she left the cottage. If she was early, she'd wait by the rocks. If she was late, she wouldn't care. She marched down the cliff path with the afternoon sun hot on her back, the sea below her swelling and falling on the shore, the gorse mustard-sharp against a royal-blue sky.

But nothing, nothing, prepared her for the moment when she looked down on the beach and saw Alex was already there holding a steaming Dancer. Where was Bo? She'd been longing to see her, especially if it was for the last time. Why had he brought Dancer? Had the dare ever been real? Or was it a stupid idea and she was the stupid American who'd suggested it?

"Well —," she whispered, the wind snatching her words. She'd go down there and call him out. She wasn't famous. Wasn't rich, or even good looking, but he didn't have the right to treat her any differently than the girls he knew.

Alex's plan for how to make the dare happen had come to him in the middle of the night. Now as he stood on the beach to give Dancer a breather, it seemed mad. Cracked. Insane. Sass had barely sat on a horse. He'd spent the entire afternoon trying to tire Dancer out, but at the jangle of tack, his brilliant horse had swung his head over his stable door with his neat ears pricked.

"Alex?"

He turned and gulped. Sass was early too. She'd had her hair done or something? It fell just past her jaw, soft flicks of hazel skimming her freckled shoulders. He'd be counting freckles when he shut his eyes. She had the sort of face, Alex decided, that didn't know if it were beautiful, but he knew. To him, she was...

Angry?

"Your hair looks good," he countered, hoping his unreliable girl radar was playing up. "You've changed it?"

"You like it?" she cut back, sharper than a knife. "Yeah, I like it." Cautious now.

"Did you really think I wouldn't find out?" "Find out what?" he stalled. Stupid.

"Don't lie to me, Alex. It's not fair." A dark bead of blood had welled up on her lip where she'd bitten it.

She knew who he was. He could see it written on her face.

"I never lied. I mean, at first, I thought you knew who I was. You're the first person I've ever met who didn't." He held his ground. It wasn't all his fault. He'd explain, if she gave him half a chance.

"What! Like the rules don't apply to you? That you're so very special because you're — royal?" She set fire to his insides.

"Since you mention it. Yes."

Her face hardened. "Oh, I'm sorry, but I've had more important things to think about than keeping up on my celebrity gossip."

Had she really just said that?

"Ah. I see. More important things! A girl on holiday who can do anything she wants; ordinary things, everyday things whenever she wants, was just curious to see how the people in the big house lived."

The look on her face made his stomach flip.

"No! You are — so wrong. I couldn't care less about how famous you are, or your house, or the rich girls you've gone out with! We got over royalty in the States a long time ago." She scoffed.

Alex tensed. She'd used "we" like she stood for a nation, the whole of America united behind her. It wasn't easy being him. He was proud of who he was, that was for sure!

"So you came all the way here just to tell me that?" He stepped into her space, breathing hard. Her hands went to his chest and she pushed him away. Dancer spooked and jerked at the reins.

"Yes! I came to say — to tell you — that I never, ever want to see you again."

Alex stared. Who was this girl to tell him to get lost? This girl who'd given him a headache since the first day they met.

"Fine! Go ahead. Don't let me stop you. You were the one who forced your way into my life."

"Don't worry, I'm gone!" And that was it. She walked away, stumbling over her feet in the sand.

Alex took Dancer's reins and vaulted into the saddle. He spurred him on and the horse kicked out, then bucked again, but Alex sent him forward. Turning for home, Dancer jumped the stream in a clatter of shingle, ignored the twisted roots and low-hanging branches on the bridle path, the scent of pine needles never sharper.

Home. As Trist loomed into view, Alex pulled Dancer up so the horse could catch his breath. He leaned forward and stroked his neck. "I'm sorry."

What else was there to say? He'd lost her. He'd let Sass go.

Sass found her way to the rocky point that overlooked the beach where she'd seen Alex galloping that first time. She didn't care who he was, only who he became when they were together. She'd gone there to find out and had finished it. Over before it began. His arrogance made her blood boil. His assumption that she was some bored girl on vacation was all wrong. And it hurt. It hurt because her heart was so sore already. This prince, or whatever he was, didn't want a girl like her. Of course he hadn't said as much, but she could see the truth now from a mile away. She'd read the rest of that magazine. He was "linked" to some other girl called Plum who wasn't ordinary, but probably beautiful, talented, and rich and wasn't empty inside. Sass lay back against a rough tussock of grass and let the tears run into her ears as above her, the sky dip-dyed blue.

A shower of pebbles plinked at her feet. That was all she needed: a sheep going *baaa* in her face. But the patter of loose shingle hadn't come from above but from the beach. In the muddled space between anger and hurt, Sass heard the sound again: a splatter of grit this time. She wriggled forward and peeked down.

It was Alex. He was back. At first, she thought he'd come on foot, but then she heard the snort of a horse: Dancer's hooves had been silenced by the sand. She slid on her backside a little closer to the edge and reached down with one foot. Withdrew it. Breathe, Sass. Breathe.

She looked again. Alex was dismounted, raking his hair back from his face. Tall. Stern. Determined. He strode over to the foot of the outcrop and looked up.

"I've come because there's so much to say, that I should have told you before." His voice, loud at first, trailed to nothing.

Sass wriggled her toes while she made up her mind. He'd come back! She counted to sixty, plus thirty seconds more. A minute and a half to choose between going forwards or back. The answer so simple in the end. What did she have to lose?

When she jumped, a leap of hope, he caught her and steadied them both. His eyes locked on hers, but she spoke first.

"So who are you then, horse boy?"

"I should have told you, Sass, but I couldn't believe that you didn't know me. And then it was too late."

"So you're a prince, for real?"

"Yeah." He pulled a face. "Alex. Alexander. Frederick. George. Second in line to the throne. Top of the family tree."

Sass wanted to laugh, it sounded so crazy.

"So your other grandma is, what? The queen?"

"Yes, my father's mother."

"Wow. Some nana."

"Yes." He paused. "She is extraordinary." Alex meant it, and something inside of Sass softened. He hadn't chosen his family, or the complicated life that came with it. He was doing the best he could, and he'd made a mistake. How could she not forgive him? It wasn't as if she had been exactly open. She stood in front of him and pressed a knuckle to his chest, as if knocking on his heart, and his arms went around her.

"My family," she whispered into his collar, "is the smallest, most stunted family tree in the whole world. More potted plant. A cactus, maybe. Spiky and in need of water." She stopped, unable to go on, and smiled, too brightly. Had he noticed? Alex pushed her back and touched the place where she'd bitten her lip earlier. His finger slid to the freckle by her mouth that she'd never hate again.

"My parents are divorcing. You've probably seen. They used to argue with each other, but now they're so bored with that, their lawyers do it for them."

"I'm so sorry. What are they like, your parents? I've seen stuff written about them…" It felt strange to ask him about his folks like they were regular people, not royalty. Though in truth, weren't they just people? And right now, Alex looked less like a prince and more like an upset boy with muddy boots and sweaty hair.

"My mother —" he paused as if he'd never discussed his parents before — "is very beautiful. She's fun. She's generous. She wants to make a difference. She needs people around her all the time. Not like me."

"And your dad?"

"He's so boring. Wants to be taken so very seriously, but if everyone just agrees with you and tells you what you want to hear, what's the point? It's not as if they're listening, are they?"

"Yes, but you don't have to be like them, do you? You can be different."

He regarded her with solemn eyes, as if it sounded possible coming from her.

"What about you, Sass? Wanting to gallop? What happened to taking things slowly?"

"No time. Bad stuff catches you if you stop too long." He looked at her and nodded, as if he sort of understood.

"Well, then, come on." Alex swung himself up on Dancer and reached down.

"What do you mean?" Sass' heart beat faster.

"You wanted to gallop, so let's do it. Only fear's holding you back. I dare you!" He beckoned with his fingers. She blinked.

"I can't. Not on Dancer! I fell off Bo."

"Nonsense." He reached down and pulled her up into the saddle. "You can hold on to me."

Without another word, she scrambled behind him. Dancer shifted uneasily with the unfamiliar weight, but Alex stroked his neck and Sass pressed closer. When the horse began jogging, Alex's hand covered hers, her fingers tightening at his touch. He whispered something. She thought he said "steady", but it might have been "ready". Oh god, he had. Too late, she felt Dancer gather himself up and then Alex let him go. She was a limpet clinging to a rock as they flew down the beach in a shower of shells, pebbles and sand, Dancer stretching ahead, his hooves on fire. Sass couldn't breathe. She couldn't cry. The months, the weeks, the days rushed by and there was only this moment, this single, incredible moment, her heart singing with every thrusting, pounding hoofbeat.

They were heading for the waves. When they reached the water's edge, Dancer snorted and thought about shying away, but Alex sat up and pulled Sass into him, kicking the horse on, and they splashed on through the sea, soaked to the skin in foam and salt spray.

At last, Alex brought Dancer back to a gentler rhythm. Sass was shaking, but she was laughing too. It felt good. So good. The best feeling in the world.

They got down and her legs gave way as she leaned into the horse to catch her breath. Side by side with Alex, their shoulders were still touching as a cat's paw of shadow came down over the beach. True to his name, Dancer spun around and they were wrenched apart. Alex only just held him.

Sass wanted to say something, but what? It was as if the invisible cord between them had snagged.

"I guess it's getting late?" was all Alex said.

"Oh!" She looked at him, winding a strand of hair around a bitten fingernail. "Yeah, I guess so — I'm kind of soaked."

Sass felt cold seawater run down her cheek and her lips begin to shiver; she couldn't let this moment go. She stepped forward, right up to Alex, until there was no space left. For a second, he seemed to just breathe her in, when all she could think about was kissing him. Sass put her hands on his waist and kept them very still. They were so close that surely he could feel her heart beating?

In reply, his fingers crept around the top of her hips, until his fingertips met over her spine. Then he was pulling her to him as if his hands had given up on directions from his brain. She closed her eyes and as he bent forward, her face tilted to his, by some instinct missing his nose. When at last they kissed, his lips were hard, then soft, and sweet, and salty-wet on hers.

"I didn't think that was going to happen," she murmured, breaking away.

"You made it happen."

"You don't mind?"

"Mmm — I still haven't quite decided; better show me again."

It was minutes later when they parted.

"Meet me here again tomorrow?" Alex's eyes held hers.

"On the beach?"

"Yes, right here in this exact spot. I command it." He squeezed her shoulders and kissed her head.

Sass paused; she couldn't. Not tomorrow. It was the wedding of Jessie and David's friends. Her heart sank.

"I can't."

"Really?" "Seriously." "Can I call you?"

"Yes! No. I — mean I have a cellphone, but it doesn't work here in England. It's not set up." It lay like a dead fish in her bedside drawer. "Besides, my uncle says there's no signal down here without climbing a hill. Do you get one where you are?"

"No, he's right. Maybe if we set out to find a signal at the same time, we might just meet in the middle?" A smile, like that was an idea.

"If you wanted to — or you had to, you could leave me a note at my uncle's gallery, do you know it? The Chapel, near the pub?"

"Snail mail, you're kidding?"

"It's —" Sass shrugged. "See it as romantic."

"Ride with me again then, after the weekend. On Monday?"

"Okay," she said, shivering, cold now the sun had gone.

"You're cold, here — have this."

He took off his sweatshirt, the one with 'WALES' on the back. "Put it on, you're shaking."

She touched the nametag sewn inside the label. Alexander Wales, it said.

"Is that your last name?"

"Kind of."

The boy with not just a name or a title, but an entire nation on his back.

And he reached forward and kissed her again.

20

STATUES ON THE LAWN

Helena looked down from her dressing-room window. In the early evening light, the garden looked almost magical, the scent of old roses drifting up through the open window, carried by the damp sea air. Statues on the lawn cast their shadows, and for a moment, Helena remembered a night when the garden was full of people. Laughing girls dressed in ball gowns and young men in uniform. It was 8 July 1943: the night of her eighteenth birthday. A band played Glenn Miller in the ballroom, everyone drank champagne and the party had spilled its way outside. She closed her eyes. The war had been the most exciting and the most terrible time of her life.

A movement brought her back to the present. What was Alexander doing? She watched him walking up the path from the beach, leading Dancer. He'd grown taller since Christmas, still had his father's critical eyes and his mother's lovely hair: Seraphina had had masses of it as a little girl. Thick, dark and a little unruly. Like her own had once been. She touched the silver hairbrush and mirror on her dressing table, her finger tracing a line in the dust. Alex had her daughter's smile ... when he smiled.

She looked out again. Her grandson was closer now. Was he whistling? She wanted to shut her eyes and remember that other time when someone else had whistled "You'll Never Know" beneath her window. She shook her head. Foolish old woman. As for Alexander, he was late for dinner.

Alex led Dancer up through the pine trees to the house, the feel of Sass filling his mind. He touched his mouth. He could still smell the scent of her skin, remember the second she stepped up and he stopped holding back. She knew about him now and it felt like the weight of a crown had been lifted off his head and chucked into the sea.

Sass knew who he was. Was angry that he hadn't told her sooner. He wasn't proud of that, but he'd wanted to get to know her first. He'd never had a chance like that before; it was always the other way around. Now he had to keep her safe from prying eyes. Away from cameras. Even down here in Cornwall, they couldn't be too careful.

Dancer neighed; they were close to home. Complicated thoughts shoved to one side, Alex stepped out. He could see the whole summer ahead: he'd take Sass swimming, they'd fish and they'd — A root across the path tripped him up and he stumbled forward. Dancer snorted. When he got to his feet and stroked the horse's neck, which had cooled at last, he saw the salt and sweat had dried to a fine white dust.

Yes, if he was careful, he and Sass could work out; starting with riding together. Bo would love to be ridden again. Trist was crisscrossed with bridle paths. There was so much of the estate that he could show her.

As Alex walked through the stable arch, he looked up at the old clock. It was a quarter to eight. He clapped a hand to his head — he'd forgotten about dinner. Ten sympathetic long faces looked over their stable doors. Alex cast around, hoping Amy could take care of Dancer.

No time to bathe and change, he stripped off his top and stuck his head under the outside tap, the cold water stinging the sunburn on his neck. Leaving Dancer with hay and water, he ran up to the house.

Amy heard the hooves from her creaky bath in the upstairs bedsit. The water was lukewarm now, but after working all day, just lying there was lovely. Bubble bath was the best. She'd get out in a minute; but out was colder than in, so she slid a bit lower until the water reached her ears.

It'd taken ages sorting the horses this evening; always did when Figgy was off. Alex had still been on the yard when she left, fiddling about and acting weird. For a while, she'd wondered if he was waiting for her, too chicken to make the first move. If he were any other boy, she'd have teased him to see where it got her. She squeezed the sponge. Why shouldn't they get together? How many girls had a chance with a boy like that, right there in front of them? He wasn't as good-looking as in his photos, or on TV, but more normal. He was still posh, but polite and nice. He liked that she flirted a bit, or at least, he used to, so what was the harm if she pushed it a bit further? Bet posh girls did that too. Girls like Plum. She'd seen pictures of her with Alex on the internet.

Amy grabbed a towel and went over to the window. She rubbed a patch in the steamed-up glass. And there he was, standing below her, half in and half out of the shadow. He'd loosened Dancer's girth and taken off his saddle. She heard the slight clink of spurs as he crouched down to check his horse's legs. The towel slipped a little as she rested her head against the window, watching him until her breath misted it up again. Alex wasn't hers and never would be. She knew it really. She sighed and turned away. Time to get dressed. Dancer had to be brushed and fed.

Sass ran the whole way back along the cliff; salt on her lips and the wind in her ears. The tingling in her veins sent her faster, until she was laughing out loud and skipping down a yellow brick road with the sun behind her.

But the road ran out. As she rounded the corner of the headland, she crashed straight into David.

"Sass! Where on earth have you been?" Her uncle was grey with worry. "We expected you back for supper two hours ago!"

She stared at him. Maybe it was because he'd burst her

bubble with what felt like a slap, but she overreacted big time. "What do you mean, where have I been?" Sass felt herself tremble. "I mean, it's not like it's dark. It's up to me where I go. Isn't it? I'm not a baby".

The words were out before she could take them back: firecrackers flipping and spitting. How could he do this right now? Spoil the moment. Play the parent. She wasn't a kid any more. She wasn't even his kid.

"You could have fallen, or drowned, or — just got lost —"

Sass turned on her heel and closed her eyes, wanting to go back where she'd come from. Wanting to stay in that moment with Alex. Galloping until she couldn't breathe, galloping until she forgot her grief. David took a step towards her.

"Come on, Sass, let's go home. You're safe and I'm sorry. I didn't mean to upset you. I'm new to all this."

"Leave me alone," she whispered, "You turn up, and I'm just supposed to go with you, and do what you say. I don't know you and I hate you. Just leave me alone." And like a baby she sat down on the path and buried her head in her knees.

Harry came over to investigate. The terrier poked his nose under her arm and licked at the salt on her hands. Harry Houdini, Potter, and Styles. She scooped him up and wiped her face, all tears and snot. He understood.

Helena huffed at Alex across the width of the polished dining table. A mile long, it gleamed in the soft light of a trembling chandelier. Dust motes spun in the air and a brass carriage clock ticked on the mantelpiece. *Tick, tick, tick.*

"You're late for dinner and you haven't bathed, or changed."

She sniffed to make her point. Alex had washed his hands by the look of him, but his clothes had the distinct whiff of salt and horse sweat.

"Sorry, Grandma." He wouldn't quite meet her eyes.

"I don't think it's too much to expect you to be on time, do you? It's so much fairer on Mrs C."

With a stiff nod to Corbett, her butler and chauffeur — the husband of her cook and housekeeper of more than forty years, Helena indicated they were ready to eat. He stepped forward. Grilled mackerel – her favourite – fished by their local man.

"Where have you been?" She spread a hard curl of butter on her bread.

"I rode down to the beach. The tide was out and I — just forgot the time," Alex stammered.

"You're honest, at least." She warmed to him a fraction. "So tell me, how was it?"

"It was —"

He flushed and looked away.

"Dear boy." Helena put down her butter knife and she reached for the long stem of her wine glass. "I can see in your face that it was glorious! Just tell me next time if you expect to be late." The crystal flashed as she tipped it to her mouth.

"Grandma?" Alex began again, lighter this time. "Gran, I was wondering — I've met someone, down at the beach, a new friend who I'd like to ride out with. If I could bring Bo in, we could ride out together. She's ridden before and loves horses. Grey ones," he added with an unnecessary flourish.

"A girl?" Helena looked down her nose, replaced her wine glass and picked up a fish knife.

"Yes." He paused. His adam's apple bobbed in his throat.

"Do we know her?" she asked, chin out, entirely the countess now.

"I'm not sure — I mean — probably not. She's from somewhere else."

Helena stared. "Somewhere else?" She lingered on the word like it was a small fish bone. She hadn't seen that coming, which was ridiculous given the number of visitors to Cornwall.

"Yes."

"I see..."

Helena dabbed her mouth with her napkin and put it down, leaving a faint trace of claret and face powder on the stiff white linen.

"No. I'm afraid not. Quite impossible. Perhaps if I knew her, but you can't go gallivanting off. I have a responsibility to your parents, as I think you know very well. Besides, Bo is a precious old thing these days and I haven't even seen this girl ride. I'm sorry, it's just the way it is."

Alex slumped a little in his chair and Helena reached across and patted his hand. "May we eat now? I'm really rather famished."

21

A TRICKLE OF SAND

Sass stuck Harry through the back door of the cottage and climbed the steps to the boat-shed loft, where she took off her damp things and sat at the edge of the bed. She hadn't meant what she said to David; it had just come out. She reached over and picked up the photo of Mom that she kept beside her pillow. It had curled in the sunlight. It wasn't a good one, but it was the last one. She was mouthing something to whoever had taken it, doing that thing with her hands that Sass couldn't make out, however much she tried. Bet it wasn't, "Hey, take another one, in case that's it." Sass put a finger to her lips and touched it.

"Mom, I kissed a prince today." Her mother would sooner believe that she'd kissed a frog.

Hearing a soft knock at the door, Sass leaned over and put the photo away.

"Who is it?"

"It's me, Jessie. Can I come in?"

"Sure..."

"I brought you some food." Jessie put down a plate of bread and cheese, and a bowl that steamed of tomato and basil.

"You didn't come by the cottage to say goodnight. David feels terrible. Is everything okay? You've been getting on so well lately."

"I know. I'm sorry, I should have, but I just wanted to be by myself."

To think about a boy, a horse and a beach.

To think of Mom.

"You two are more alike than you know. Did you have a bad day?"

"No. It was — kind of perfect."

Jess looked so puzzled by her answer that Sass wanted to explain. She had to tell someone.

"I found a horse." She began. "A silver one. Like in your painting."

"Which painting?" Jessie sat down beside her.

"That one." She pointed at the dream horses by her bed. "The one you've been fixing up by that artist, Lucy someone."

"And?"

Sass paused. How much she should tell her? Alex was a secret she wanted to hug, but it blurted out. Some of it. "Then I met a boy from the estate who was riding on the beach and we got talking."

"You met a boy this evening from Trist?" For all her laid-backness, Jessie looked surprised.

Sass didn't fill in the in-between.

"Yes."

"Is — is he nice?" Jessie asked carefully.

"Yeah, he's my age and he's really good with horses."

"That's nice, then?" Jessie grinned. "Is that why you forgot to come home?"

"Yeah. Kind of." Sass felt herself redden. "I — I really like him and I think he likes me." She fiddled with a trickle of sand in her pocket. She could hardly believe it was true.

"Okay, I understand now, Sass, but take it slow. You have all the time in the world."

Sass gazed into Jessie's kind, open face and nodded, but inside she felt just the opposite. If she'd learned anything over the past few months, it was that no one had all the time in the world. Life could change in a smash of glass and a crump of car metal.

Plum rammed the lid of the suitcase closed and sat on it. She couldn't wait any longer for Alex to call; she'd make up his mind for him. Go visit, pop by. He was only in Cornwall, not halfway across the world. Cee-Ce's new boyfriend had a yacht down there and the pair were going tomorrow for a long weekend. She'd cadge a lift with them. Alex could hardly turn her down, and the rest would be easy.

She'd chosen what to wear already. Short shorts or her white jeans, depending on the weather, with a cheeky Breton sailor top and a pair of high wedges. Bosie wouldn't notice them gone. And she must take her yellow Hunters to brighten up a field. Alex had lots of fields. He was always banging on at school about the sea or his horses. Well, she could do coast and country too. It wouldn't kill her.

The biggest drag was that she'd be stuffed in the back of the Porsche. Give it a couple of years and things would be different. She and Alex would be driving; they could have the roof down and then she wouldn't mind about her hair. Oh god, sunglasses ... which ones?

Plum had been to Cornwall once before she met Alex: a Discovery Sailing Week with the school. How anyone "discovered" they liked sailing was beyond her. Total nightmare. She'd arrived with her suitcase expecting a big boat ... or at least one with a motor. Instead, it had been the windy type. An old wooden ship with real sails. The wind had blown and the sea had frothed, although the heeling wasn't the worst part; that was quite fun. It wasn't even the tacky thing either. "Going about," as one of the boys had excitedly explained — after she thought he'd asked her out. No. It was the nausea. Everybody had been so seasick, except for her and the crew. She'd had to sit there, zigzagging pointlessly up and down the coast in a stained orange lifejacket listening to them all chuck up. It was more disgusting than a public toilet.

This time, she'd be in charge. She'd get past "hello" and then casually mention how awkward it was playing gooseberry to Cee-ce and whatshisname. Alex would invite her to stay at his grandmother's huge place and history would be made.

Her only worry, if she had any, was his parent thing. The divorce. She wouldn't want it to get in the way. Alex had been so cut up, rushing off from school. She'd understood – it had happened to her – but you got used to it by the third time around. There were even some advantages. Not many, but a few.

Finally, there was Cressida Slater. What to do about her? Plum stabbed at the journalist's name next to the gossip column spread out beside her. Should she tell her that she was going? Then if Cressida — Plum supposed — happened to be down there with a photographer, well...

It was why she had to get what she was wearing exactly right.

22

THE WEDDING PARTY

Sass gazed at the scarlet slippers in her hand and felt momentarily homesick. She'd bought them one long, hot, sticky afternoon in Chinatown. So hot, New York was suffocating. You sweated doing nothing. She and Mom had taken the subway to Canal Street to go shopping. They loved going there and if they got too hot, they'd tuck inside a store with air conditioning. It was how she came to buy these. Slip-ons. Made in Hong Kong. Only five dollars in cotton and plastic, but the sun had glittered on the sequins on the front and Mom said she'd buy them.

Afterwards, they'd had dim sum: those perfect steamed dumplings. Half the time, you didn't know what was inside them: pork, or prawn or vegetable. You just pointed and a cranky waiter would toss down a basket and scribble a Chinese character on the bill. It might have been a word, or a number, the whole guessing was the fun of it. She paused and gathered her thoughts; life was so random. Look at how she'd met Alex. A prince in clover? Ha-ha. You couldn't make it up. He was so stuffy and British, but then, when he kissed her, he really kissed her; he hadn't stopped kissing her till her breath ran out.

Sass sighed. Alex wouldn't get to kiss her today. It was the wedding of Jessie and David's friends and no getting out of it.

"It's only up the road, at a local church, no distance at all. You can wear your new dress. They'll ring the bells and there'll be wedding cake and fizz, and a jazz band." Jessie had been firm. "It'll be good for you to dress up."

Sass had put on the Daphne dress. It was lovely, but it itched at the back, and the shoes Jessie lent her had been three sizes too small; they were like Bigfoot and Bambi, which was why the red slippers were out. She slid her feet into them now and scrunched her toes hard. No Alex today. And not tomorrow either. But on Monday ... She tapped her toes together and let the thrill run through her.

Alex had slept in. He sat up and swung his legs out of the bed, which creaked in protest. He'd been hot and kicked off his sheets and they lay in a tangled heap. What time was it? He reached for his phone. Useless for anything else without a signal. Glancing at the palm of his hand, he saw where he'd scribbled the name of Sass's uncle's gallery, The Chapel, last night. He closed his fingers around the ink.

It was past nine and bright daylight had long since crept around the curtains that had hung there all his life. He yawned and fell back on the bed, running a hand across his chest. What was Sass doing now? He could picture her on Bo, mud on her face and her hair blowing loose. He liked her: "I really, really like her!" He said again to the ceiling.

Sass was the summer he didn't want to end. His secret for as long as he could keep it.

The wedding was held in the smallest church Sass had ever seen. No bigger than a shoebox stuffed with coloured tissue. It felt miles away down a winding lane by the shore of an inlet where a bunch of small boats lay stranded in the mud, waiting for the sea to roll in. Seabirds with long beaks pecked at slippery rocks and a sour smell of drying seaweed hung in the air. It was hot and still, and packed; standing room only at the back. Guests stood chatting outside until the organist struck up and the bride arrived, pink-faced in a swirl of tulle, trailing two small, glowering flower girls.

Sass closed her eyes and concentrated; she imagined she was at Eddie's Ices. She swallowed and took a deep breath. It was no good; instead of cooling her down, her nine-year-old self was picking the nuts off a cherry-vanilla sundae with extra whipped cream. A tower of milky sweetness that made her feel sick, but she had to keep going because it was Mom's special treat. She couldn't remember why.

Sass forced herself to look up from the narrow pew and the people crushing her on either side. Hymns were being sung. Prayers done. A sudden hush had descended for the vows. A bead of sweat rolled past her ear and down her neck.

Breathe, Sass, breathe. The minister was droning on … and on, and on.

"I am required to ask anyone present who knows a reason why these persons may not lawfully marry, to declare it now…"

She was back in that other church, everyone in black for Mom's funeral.

"Ashes to ashes, dust to dust…"

What was that smell? Was it the flowers? Sass's hand flew to her mouth and she rushed out through the side door of the church and leaned heavily against a headstone. In the shade of a yew tree, she bent over and took a gulping breath. Don't puke. Concentrate. She heaved.

"My dear girl, can I help you?" It was an elderly English lady in stout laced shoes, a tweed skirt and a green quilted jacket. She held out a large spotted handkerchief that Sass took gratefully. She wiped her face and blew her nose, offering it back to the woman, who shook her head, motioning her to keep it with a flicker of her fingers.

"I'm okay. Really. I just needed some air."

"Was it so very romantic?" the old lady inquired in a voice that suggested she didn't think so.

"No — I mean, it was lovely. It's just — I'm not feeling so well."

"Ah, I see…" The woman was more sympathetic. "One never knows how these things will go. I'm here to see the family."

"Are you bride or groom?" Sass asked, wanting to be polite. "Oh no, my dear, they're all dead and buried. When you get to my age, you find yourself almost quite alone, but it gets easier, and here, they're never far away." She gestured vaguely in the direction of a line of elaborate marble headstones on a raised area that looked out across mudflats to the water beyond.

"Shall we sit down? I have a thermos of tea." It was more of a command than a suggestion.

The lady sat down at one end of a nearby bench with Sass at the other. She twisted the top off a steaming flask and carefully poured a plastic cupful that they shared between them for a few minutes.

"What's your name, dear?" "It's Sass. Saskia Emerson."

"You're an American?"

"Yes, from New York. I'm here for the summer. Maybe longer."

"Are you staying nearby?"

"Not far away. And yourself?" Sass thought she should ask. "Oh, I'm from these parts. Born and bred." She gestured in the vague direction of everywhere. Not that she could mean that. The old lady continued. "Did you know that during the war thousands of Americans were based here?" Her voice went a little fierce, as if they were all clustered on this one spot.

"No, I didn't."

"For D-Day. Most of them, at least. Officers billeted, other ranks in tents in fields and woods."

Her face had taken on a distant look. She had to be really old because the war was so long ago. Sass had never met anyone who was in it.

"How old were you then?" The question asked itself. How rude was she? But the woman reached over and patted her hand. She looked into Sass's face as if she saw something important there.

"Not much older than you are now, my dear." And she rose stiffly to her feet.

"Where's your mother? You've not been well."

It was as though someone had sucked the last oxygen from the air and Sass thought she might faint. She shook her head as her answer caught in her throat with a choking sound that seemed to come from someone else.

"Mom's dead," she blurted out. The bitter words lay there in a cold puddle of sick.

The woman's face clouded over; that or the sun went in. Every part of Sass felt limp.

"Oh my dear, I'm so very sorry —" She had just reached out and put a liver-spotted hand on Sass's when Jessie appeared around the side of the church.

"Sass! Are you all right, my love? I saw you rush out, but I couldn't move."

The old lady interrupted, a little sharply.

"She's been sick. I wonder, should I drive her home?"

Jessie looked at the lady, her eyes widening and Sass felt her own shoulders sag in relief: they knew each other and she could go home without ruining everyone's day.

"Er — yes, of course," Jessie stammered. "If that's what Sass wants, or as soon as the service is over, we're happy to take her?"

"Really, there's no need. My car is here. She just needs rest and shade. It's awfully stuffy today."

Sass's rescuer waved an aged hand at the church gate and a gleaming car slid into view as a peal of church bells rang out over the water.

Cressida had taken the call from the fruitily awful Plum Benoist and was on her way to Cornwall. A new royal angle at last. Teeth clamped around a cigarette, she negotiated the final stomach-curling hairpin bend in her black Gucci Fiat 500 with its go-faster green and red stripe. She screeched as an inch of ash fell in her lap. Flinging her "poison stick" out, she narrowly missed the windscreen of a knackered old Bentley that had pulled over to let her pass.

Her new assignment had begun on "*Prince A*" and "*Miss B*". The Benoist girl had been most forthcoming, letting slip with the subtlety of a scalpel that she'd be visiting her annointed boy today.

Cressida had sent a photographer ahead, a smooth-talking paparazzo called Silvio on a Ducati motorbike. She was staying up the road from the ancestral pile at some dreary pub: The Smugglers, or The Strugglers. Someone would swing for it, if there wasn't any Wi-Fi. Sightings of the young royal were rare. She knew because she'd followed him for long enough. Photos of the handsome young pup "in love"? Worth a bomb. All grown up now: he was fair game.

23

ROCKING THE BOAT

Alex pulled on beach shorts and an old T-shirt. It was too hot to ride. It was too hot to do anything. All the horses were out in the fields and the yard was deserted, except for Susan, who lay fast asleep in the shade. He walked up to see the foals in the cool of their walled paddock; it had been a kitchen garden once. Alex had seen grainy photos of young under-gardeners holding up pineapples, back before the First World War. There had been no pineapples since. No under-gardeners either. And no prizes now for guessing which foal was Bo's. She was the colour of a storm cloud with the flash of white on her forehead, and the cheekier of the two. All legs and ears, and a stubby tail. Quality, he noted. He expected nothing less.

The foals stuck together, jostling for position. At six months, they'd been weaned from their mothers, but they soon got used to it. Alex remembered how, when he was seven, he'd shivered in the dorm on his first night at prep school. In the end it hadn't been that bad; it was later that he hated it, when his friends began to treat him differently. He'd stuck with a few mates, but it wasn't exactly fair on them. Who wanted to hang out with him and a policeman?

With a playful squeal, Bo's filly nipped her field mate and charged to the end of the small paddock. With a watch-me toss of her head, she trotted back as if treading on air and made him smile. Shook him out of his apathy like someone else he could think of. Alex grinned and leaned against the gate. What should he do today if he wasn't seeing Sass? She'd come into his life and mucked it about, and he liked it. Resting his head on his arms, he rolled a stone with his toe. This feeling ... These mixed-up feelings he was trying to work out. What he was beginning to feel for her was like nothing else.

The Porsche purred past the tombstone-like sign to Trist and through the ornate, rusted gates that ground open, seemingly on their last legs.

"Ow!" moaned Plum as she bumped her head on the roof for the millionth time that journey.

"Shut up, can't you!" hissed her sister, loud enough to be heard in London. "We're here now."

"Whoa," said Cee-ce's boyfriend at the wheel: Brad, an American, who worked in finance. Plum craned her neck but couldn't see anything, praying that the house was more impressive than its entrance.

They crawled up through a park of overgrown fields until they turned a wide curve and she saw it for the first time. Shabbier than she'd imagined, with a worn-out face that looked like it could do with surgery.

Brad revved the engine and parked in a spray of gravel. "That's awesome," Brad said, while Plum pressed her temples; the beginnings of a headache. Her sister had totally lied about how much Brad earned, if he was this impressed already.

They got out, Cee-Ce making a thing of dragging out Plum's suitcase like it was time for them to leave already. Plum looked around. The place looked abandoned, or haunted, and where was Alex? She'd sent him a text and he still hadn't replied.

"Can I help you?"

She glared straight into the un-made-up face of a girl about her own age, maybe older, seventeen or eighteen. She wasn't much taller than Plum and had a definite farmer's tan. It stopped at the neck and arms of her too-tight polo top that had shrunk in the wash. She had sweaty patches under her armpits, a pigtail of strawberry-blonde hair left to bleach in the sun and, worst of all, she was wearing filthy jodhpurs, and Crocs, the ugliest shoes ever invented. A stable girl? Phew. Plum sighed inwardly. At least she wasn't competition.

"Yes, I'm looking for — Alexander." She'd dispensed with his title. In her head, they were beyond that. "Is he home?"

"Yeah, he's up with the foals, but I expect he'll be down soon. Her Ladyship is out." The girl eyed her with the sort of sleepy-eyed look boys liked.

Plum noted the cobbles. "Shall I wait here? Or go straight up to the house?" She wasn't breaking an ankle on those.

"Plum!" Alex came striding over. "What on earth are you doing here?" He went to kiss her cheek, but she wobbled at the wrong moment, and he missed.

"Thought I'd surprise you. Aren't you pleased?" She flipped her hair to one side.

Behind his back, Plum narrowed her eyes at her sister, cringing when Brad rushed forward without waiting to be introduced, his hand outstretched like a paddle. Alex shook it with a slight tightening of his jaw.

"We were on our way sailing," she fibbed with practiced ease. "And thought we'd pop by." She flapped a hand in Ceece's direction. "This is my sister, Cerise — and her fiancé, Brad. It's his boat."

Her sister arched an eyebrow and smiled sourly in reply, tapping her watch at Plum when Alex wasn't looking.

Plum glanced at her prince. He had the same shadowed look on his face that she'd seen at the ball. He didn't seem at all happy that she was there.

"Right," he said, making a special effort to be polite. "I see you've met Amy?"

Alex smiled gratefully in the other girl's direction and she smirked back. Plum felt a sudden urge to slap her, but made do with studying Alex instead.

He looked tanned and his hair had grown. It almost curled at the sides. He was looking good, much nicer than she remembered, but her plan wasn't working. She hadn't expected him to whip off his shirt and lay it like a cloak across puddles, but he could look slightly more enthusiastic.

Urgh. A hairy muzzle thrust its way into her crotch. A slobbering dog. She kneed the wet nose away, her white jeans ruined.

At least Alex seemed to cheer up.

With an infuriating grin, he clicked his fingers to call the dog away. "My grandmother's out, but I expect I can rustle up some tea. Follow me."

He led them through a back door into a vast kitchen where an old Aga simply radiated heat. Cee-ce looked like she might pass out.

"It's our cook, Mrs C's, day off: Saturday, you see," Alex said, as if that explained anything. Back in London, their housekeeper, Marta, worked 24-7.

"I think there's cake in the tin." He prised off a rusted floral lid.

"No, really!" She and Cee-Ce both cried out in sisterly union, shrinking from a sweet waft of strawberry and vanilla. Bad carbs and sugar: an absolute no-no.

"Sure. Don't mind if I do." Brad the bear that needed feeding.

Plum crept up to Alex while he filled the kettle. "You didn't answer my texts." Tugging gently at the edge of his T-shirt.

"I'm afraid we don't get a signal down here. And I —"

"Wow! Not even Wi-Fi?" Plum was shocked.

"No hot water, either." Alex replied. "If you want a shower, you have to catch the boiler unawares."

Plum felt a little faint. It was the hottest day of the year. She had a headache and had been perspiring all morning in the back of a Porsche. She tried her best to pretend it didn't matter, channelling what she'd learned from her sisters.

"But you do have lots of lovely fresh air." The fat black dog slumped at her feet farted loudly, with a rumble that sounded like thunder.

"I thought you hated the country?" Alex looked at her. The intensity of his gaze was confusing. She was used to boys looking at her in awe, but this was different.

"What's not to like?" she lied.

"Milk and sugar?"

"No, no. Green tea if you've got it?" She reached forward and plucked a piece of straw from his hair. It stuck to her fingers. Eew.

"I think we're all out."

"Earl Grey?" And stared askance as Alex handed her a mismatched cup and saucer — and it was then that she saw what was written on his palm. She craned closer.

He hadn't seen her looking, his hand falling to his side. But she'd seen the name: Sass Chapel.

It twisted like a pinch. Who was she? Not the girl she'd just met? No, that was a Same-y Amy.

"I'm sorry, Plum," Alex began, looking uncomfortable. He tugged her to the corner of the room. "I'm sorry that you've come all the way down here. I never meant to lead you on. You've been — um — more than a good friend to me. You look fantastic — I mean, look at you, you could have any boy and they're all jealous as hell of me, but I'm not the one for you."

Plum twisted her hair; the disappointment in her chest was surprising.

"Silly! I never thought that for a moment. I've always known we're just — crew. I'm your cox, remember?"

She leaned up on tiptoe and brushed his cheek with hers, her nails curled tight, tight, in her palms. When she unclenched them in the back of the car later, they bled a little. An important lesson. If anything in life goes wrong, take it out on someone else.

When Cressida Slater's message came a little later, Plum was so ready to kiss and tell.

Sass's jaw dropped. The car parked outside the church was very big and sleek, and some old guy in a peaked cap stood holding the door open. She looked around. If he was waiting for the bride, he'd got the wrong girl. She slid into the backseat, which creaked softly, the cream leather worn smooth, noting a velvet carpet on the floor that she hoped not to get sick on. On the opposite side from her, the old lady stooped and got in too, with the driver's hand at her elbow. She looked across at Sass.

"I realise you must have no idea who I am." She smiled drily. "How very rude of me to presume. Please call me Helena."

The car swept out of the churchyard in a crunch of stones and turned smoothly onto the country lane. Behind them, the wedding party was closing in a noisy ring of confetti and camera flashes.

"Thank you so much," Sass said. "I think my uncle and Jessie thought a wedding would be fun."

"In my experience, and I have only ever done it once myself, weddings are a necessary nuisance. A public show, that's all. Secrecy is so much more exciting. Now, my dear girl, where am I taking you?"

Sass was utterly tongue-tied. Who was this extraordinary woman? She acted like a Hollywood star from one of Mom's old black-and-white movies. Maybe she was one, once?

"Honestly, you don't need to drive me all the way. I can get out and walk before long."

"Really, it's no trouble. Humbug?"

"Excuse me?"

"Travel sweet. To settle your stomach?" She held out a small round tin.

"Sure — thank you." Sass sucked on the hard, sharp mint, wishing for all she was worth that she was alongside the driver with the window wound down, because a car like this wasn't meant for these roads, or for old movie stars in tweed; you could keep it for rock stars — or royalty.

Plum and her poisonous sister had left more than an hour ago and Alex was still restless. He'd seen them off down the drive and kept walking. Head down, arms pumping. Plum had put him in a stinking mood. Okay, he'd disappointed her. He felt bad, but it wasn't as if he'd encouraged her. Just seeing her was a jarring reminder that summer would soon be over, and then it'd be back to reality, whatever that meant for him.

He reached the front gates, his "permitted" limit unless he wanted the hassle of a new minder sooner. Coming up the road was the unmistakable growl of a powerful car. Not the Porsche back again? His heart sank. Instead, Grandma's old Bentley swept past: a gleam of racing green heading for the village. It was only a glimpse, but he could have sworn that Sass was sitting in the back. No, that was ridiculous. He was seeing things. Sweat in his eyes. He wiped his face on his arm.

His request at dinner about wanting to ride out with a friend had been dismissed. Grandma had made it quite plain that was never going to happen. No girl, he suspected, was good enough for him in his grandmother's eyes, and certainly not one he'd just met. Ironic, given that his mother wanted him to meet just about every girl in *Vogue*.

He'd choose his own friends, or none at all.

Alex squinted against the sun, trying for the life of him to imagine a scenario in which Sass came back to Kensington and they could be together. He could show her the sights of London; they could ride the red buses and be tourists for a day.

And that, he knew, was the lie of it. The difficult but inescapable truth was that hidden in Cornwall, they could be themselves. Nowhere else. He didn't doubt that he more than liked her, but beyond this summer, others would get in the way; people would talk and she wouldn't fit. Wrong class, wrong voice, wrong look, wrong nationality. It was the way things were. This was his life.

He strode on, the heat of the tarmac burning through his flip-flops, the air thick with insects: dozy wasps and the whine of flies. The press would follow her, and she'd hate it. Unlike Plum, who'd suck it up like an ice-cold Coke through a straw.

His mouth ran dry as he remembered the last time he'd made headlines. The First VIII had qualified for the Nationals in May, the biggest school rowing event before Henley. As stroke, it was his job to set the pace while Plum steered the line and the rest of the guys pulled like fury.

Hands, body, slide. The boat cutting through the water.

Except that he'd set a rate they couldn't possibly keep up, as if he'd had something to prove. He remembered the strain in his arms, shutting his eyes with the effort, and the sudden disastrous skew as he caught "a crab", when his blade stuck in the water, his oar wrenched above his head. The boat had rocked to an awful stop in the wash of their rivals.

"Nice one, Alex," Gully had grunted. "Epic. Nearly tipped us in. We're out of it now."

The headlines had been blunter:

NATIONALS DISASTER. NO HEIR IN THE TANK. PRINCE BLOWS UP!

Alex looked up at the sky; a dark cloud was smothering the blue. He wanted to be with Sass. They were good together, but he had to think. Common sense and duty demanded dullness. Besides, she wouldn't want to be with him for long. She just didn't know it yet.

At the crossroads, instead of heading back to Trist, he found himself hacking his way down an overgrown short cut to the beach, slashing at the nettles and thorns. He wanted waves; he wanted water. He wanted to feel the cold pull of the sea.

And then he'd decide what to do next.

24

A BEACON OF LIGHT

When the car reached the top of the hill, Sass had insisted palely on getting out. She'd spent the last few minutes of the journey under Helena's firm guidance, breathing in through her nose and out through her mouth.

"Thank you for the ride, but I'm okay now. I can walk the rest of the way."

"If you're sure, my dear — I suppose the air will do you good." A quiet understanding had passed between them.

Sass stood in the narrow lane. It was so hot. Frills of giant ferns lined the steep road, sprouting from dry-stone walls that must have taken hundreds of years to build. From where she stood, she could taste the sea, a sharp tang of salt above the clammy air, but she wanted to see it too. To feel a breeze. A farm track on her left led up to higher ground. Sass took it, her silk dress clinging damply to her legs.

It continued up across a wheat field, and it was from the top of the slope that she saw him in the distance, or rather, the back of him. It was Alex, wasn't it?

He was about half a field in front of her and striding ahead. Tall and tanned, his shorts low slung. She called out to him, but he was too far away to hear her. She forgot her nausea as Helena's words stole into her head: "Secrecy is so much more exciting." She'd follow him and surprise him instead.

It was a struggle to keep up, Sass wasn't dressed for stalking. The coarse grass, spiky gorse and brambles snatched at her dress, but just when she'd had enough, they came out on the coast path and Sass recognised where she was. Below her stretched the beach. Their beach. It was smaller now, shrinking with the incoming tide. Not that she'd ever understood the tide thing. How could so much water come and go because of the moon? Some stuff was way bigger than she was.

Sass looked ahead, shading her eyes from the glare. Alex was still marching along. Where the path wound down to the sand, he kicked off his flip-flops. First one, then the other, hopping to keep his balance. Then he began pulling off his shirt, chucking it to one side as he headed for the water. Watching from the shore, Sass's eyes crept across his back. Lean and smooth-skinned, his arms and back were tight-knotted like wood, and gleamy with sweat. With a last burst of speed, he ran into the water, the waves rushing up to meet him. It was all Sass could do to stand there.

Alex dived straight into the swell. He came up gasping at the sudden cold. It felt really good. He turned on his back for a few strokes, kicking hard. Putting his feet down, he looked back at the shore.

"What. . .?"

He wiped his face and looked again, and shoved his hair out of his eyes, which were stinging from the sea. Sass was standing on the beach, ankle-deep in the shallows, holding up the edge of her dress from the surf. His heart beat harder, his chest going in and out, until all thoughts of ending what he'd started were washed from his mind. He knew he had to find a voice from somewhere.

"Truth or Dare?" he called, delivered with a coolness he didn't feel. He cupped a hand to his ear for her answer, and it came back loud and clear.

"Dare!" She was smiling. Hand on hip now, slightly lopsided, her hem trailing in the water.

"I dare you to come in!"

"No way! I don't have a bathing suit!" She gestured at her dress. "Take it off. I won't look. I promise!"

She hovered for a second as if making up her mind. "Turn around, then," she called.

Alex obeyed, holding his nose comically as he ducked under the water, and suddenly, she was alongside him, catching her breath, splashing and laughing. Treading water, their feet and knees bumped.

"How did you know where to find me?"

"I followed you," she said. Tentative now. "I got back early from the wedding and saw you in the distance. I called out, but you didn't hear me."

Her eyes were sparkling. She made his head spin. It was that or the freezing water.

"Maybe I was just pretending not to hear you."

She cocked her head to the side. "And why would you do that?" He grinned. "So I could do this." He scooped up a handful of water and went to splash her, but with a duck dive and a flick of her toes, she swam out of reach. Coming up for air, Sass switched to her back, flicking water with her pointed toes.

"You'll have to catch me first!" She was a good swimmer.

But so was he.

Afterwards, Sass sat with her knees drawn up, as they dried off in the shelter of the cliff. The dull sickness had gone, replaced by a bright feeling that nothing else existed. She was a beacon across water, her every sense lit from this one rocky spot.

She stole a glance at Alex, who was leaning back on his elbows with a physical ease that was at odds with his normal reserve. She wondered how many people got to know him like this, then remembered there was another side to him she'd never seen. Alexander, second in line to the British throne. She couldn't imagine it. All she knew about that world came from history, gossip and TV.

"Alex? How did this happen?" "What?"

"This. Y'know. Us?"

"Beats me." He grinned across at her. "Perhaps I have a thing for American girls who don't know a prince when they see one." He reached over and pulled her to him, so she was resting her head against his shoulder. "So how come you can swim like a fish?"

Sass opened her eyes, suddenly aware of the subject they were circling. "I started swimming lessons really young. My mom made me train hard. . ." Her voice trailed away and the sand beneath her seemed to sink a little deeper.

"Well, you're bloody good."

Whoosh. The moment to tell him about Mom came and went.

"Thanks," she said. "But tell me something more about you. What's your life like — away from Trist and the horses?"

"I don't think about it. I just get on with being who I am. Born that way. Like having freckles."

"I hate having those."

"That's tough because I like them very much, especially that one." He touched her face.

"But it's hard, right? Having all that responsibility?"

"Yes, and no. It's a privilege, just one that I don't feel ready for. It's just me, you see, making it up?"

"At least nobody gets to vote you out!"

"Don't get me wrong, I'm not complaining, not really. I have help, but my mistakes, my personal mistakes, don't go unnoticed. They get picked over, twisted and turned by the press until they become these monsters."

"So you hide," she said softly, "down here in Cornwall?"

A pulse was beating at his temple.

She hadn't meant to put it so tactlessly; she knew how it felt to hide.

He was frowning. "I'm *me* down here. I don't want any special treatment."

146

Sass swallowed, wanting to make things right. "I know. I'm just saying that I understand what it's like to feel lonely even when you're surrounded by people."

She scrunched her face at the memory of an SUV riding the kerb of a city street. The wail of a hundred sirens. People. Lots of people.

Alex had seen. He walked over to where she'd stepped out of her dress: a puddle of silk on the sand. Gathering it up, he brought it over to her. It wasn't like she was naked in her underwear, but Sass felt suddenly self-conscious. How come underwear didn't feel like a bikini? One felt like freedom and the other a secret. She shook her dress out and slipped it on, a shell of mother-of-pearl around her freckled skin.

"I'm starving," Alex announced, wrapping his arm around her waist. "Are you?"

"Yes!"

"What shall we eat?"

"Chocolate and pizza. Together. Right now. Can you snap your fingers?"

Alex laughed. "Sorry! That's something else I can't do." "What? Princes aren't allowed to eat pizza?"

"No. Go out for pizza."

"Hey, it's overrated, but you can do chocolate, right?"

"Our cook, Mrs C, makes the best chocolate cake in the world."

Alex had a chef? Of course he did. Sass tried not to look surprised.

"Hey, nothing compares to the humble American brownie. We invented those and they're the best."

"I beg to differ, madam." Alex did a curly thing with his hand and bowed, all musketeer.

"So. . ." Sass wrinkled her nose. "Being a prince isn't just cake, palaces and shaking hands with presidents?"

Alex reached across and shook her hand.

"Feel that? Years of practice, but yes, that's correct."

She felt the grip, then the rub of his thumb. He turned her palm over, kissed her knuckles and looked up.

"So shall we go out next week? Ride, I mean. Why stop at one gallop on the beach?"

Sass gulped.

He grinned. "On Monday? Me on Dancer. You on Bo."

"Yes, yes. I'd love that."

They were close. So close.

"Early?"

Brown eyes tugging her to him.

"Early," she breathed.

"You won't say anything to anyone, will you?"

He traced her collarbone with a fingertip.

"No. Nothing! Who would I tell?"

"We can't be too careful. Believe me, I know."

Sass opened and shut her mouth. A tiny last fish gasp, caught on the end of a line.

Neither heard the click and whir of a camera, or saw the photographer slip away like a snake in the grass.

25

FAMILY TIES

Alex walked back up to Trist. He couldn't wait for Monday. He didn't care what Grandma thought. Bo would look after Sass and he'd look after Bo. That was all that mattered.

The grey mare had been small for a jump-racer, not much bigger than a pony. She'd had courage and, in her day, she'd been the best: a champion. They all rode; it was in the blood. His other grandmother loved flat racing best. He hadn't seen her since his parents' split, but she sent him old-fashioned notes on thick gold-crested paper. As girls, his grandmothers had been friends, but something had happened that couldn't be discussed, and now they didn't speak.

Making his way up the back stairs to his bedroom, he stepped out of his wet shorts, towelled his hair and pulled on tracksuit bottoms. He threw open the window and climbed out. He wanted to look back at the sea. Nothing could ruin his good mood.

Alex heard it before he saw it. The distinctive whirr of rotor blades in the distance. Visitors. He groaned: not twice in one day. A black private-charter helicopter buzzed into view and hovered like a persistent horsefly. It landed on the front lawn, blowing up a mound of mown grass that the gardener, Roberts, had raked up that morning. Three people stepped out, stooping under the revolving blades: his mother in white, holding on to a large hat, a smug-looking polo player and a man in a suit with a long face, and two briefcases. Not good. Polo guy and his mother walked up the front steps, laughing as they went. He noticed how she leaned into him. Why didn't she ever come to Trist on her own? Deflated, Alex slumped, his feet dangling, but eventually he had to go in. Not wanting to see her with the others, he waited almost until dinner before knocking on her door.

"Come."

She was sitting at her dressing-table mirror in a silky dressing gown with droopy sleeves, struggling with the clasp of a gold and diamond bracelet. It was impossible to be angry with her; she was his mum.

She looked up. "Darling, it's you! I wondered where you were." Discarding her jewellery, she held out her arms.

Who else was she expecting? Alex let himself be engulfed by her perfume. Chanel. He remembered the name from the jars and bottles in her dressing room back in Kensington. When he was little, he'd sneak out of bed and fall asleep on the landing floor waiting for his parents to come home.

"What have you been doing? You've grown so much in the last few months. Almost a man."

He wanted to tell her; there was so much he could say, but he paused too long and she filled the space with chatter.

"It's been so awful in town since it got out about Daddy and me. Paparazzi everywhere. I can't even have a quiet dinner at L'Auberge any more. I've simply thrown myself into work."

She looked thinner. She always looked thin but this time she was the size of a stick insect. The pressure his father was putting her under wasn't fair. It would be so easy to break her.

"You're here now, Mum. You can relax, no one will follow you." He meant it. He'd look after her.

"Oh lord, darling." Her eyes flashed. "I'm not staying here; this place would simply kill me. I'd die of boredom. I just wanted to come and see you, and Mother. A flying visit." Her laugh sounded like a twig snapping.

"So who's that with you, then?" Alex asked, an edge in his tone.

"Don't be cross. I've brought Eduardo to meet you. He's the most marvellous polo player. I expect you've heard of him. He trounced your father a few weeks ago. I thought it would be a treat; he's terribly suave and a little homesick for Argentina. Oh, and the other one is Michael Balding, bit of a bore. A lawyer."

"What's he here for, to sell Trist?" He didn't want to think about the other thing. The Divorce.

"Naughty. You know very well, nothing has been decided,

but all this…" She waved her hand around the room. "Is just too much for Grandma and you won't want to be buried down here for ever, because let's not forget…" She paused with a bittersweet smile. "One day, you'll have your other, rather larger inheritance, as your father's son."

He gazed at her hard. She was right, Trist would be hers to sell, not that he could imagine Grandma ever gone.

A shadow of doubt crossed his mother's face and she reached out and touched his arm.

"Alex, darling, how have you been? I miss you so much when you're away. Have you been dreadfully bored on your own with just Grandma?"

She didn't get it. She really didn't. He chose to be here.

His mother looked up at him with her hooded eyes. He caved for a second, and just as he was about to try to explain, she flicked her attention away. A split second when she could have waited and listened.

"I heard you behaved rather dreadfully with your father the other day?" Triumph in her voice.

"Yes," he said coolly, more than he felt. "I told him what I thought of him: you, school — everything."

Her fleeting sympathy was replaced by the tip-tap of her nails and then the stab and swish of a make-up brush.

Helena, Countess of Tremayne, watched Seraphina, her lovely, selfish daughter, drop a bomb on her son. They were sitting in the drawing room after dinner, Helena smoking one of her rare, gold-tipped cigarettes by the open French windows.

Eduardo the Argentine had gone up, exhausted by his own ego, and Seraphina had taken off her heels. Barefoot, she seemed slighter, although her fragility was an illusion only men fell for. She loved her daughter, but Helena was no fool. Seraphina had shimmered at dinner in topaz satin, the centre of attention like the prima donna she always was. Helena wondered if the price of such attention would prove too much.

"Alex, my darling, I have something to ask you —" Seraphina began softly at first and then, when she failed to catch his attention "— to tell you." She frowned, the lines on her forehead unnaturally faint.

"What is it?" Alex replied. He cared. Helena could see it written on his face, although he tried to cover up and pretend he didn't.

"We'd like you to come back to London. Daddy and I. We have to make a formal announcement and may need you there for a friendly photocall."

Hardly a family day out, was Helena's immediate thought.

Alex's face simply dropped. "What announcement?"

"Darling. The divorce. I'm afraid it's happening. It's being announced officially. Decree nisi."

Alex looked confused, then hurt and finally furious. "Well, you don't need me, then, do you?"

"I need you; you're my strength." She looked up at him from under her lashes. A skill that she'd practised since she was a child.

"And Father?"

"He needs you too. You're his son and heir."

"I see. . ."

Alexander stood there helplessly for a few seconds; then he turned on his heel and left, slamming the door behind him so hard that the photographs on the shelves fell down.

"Darling, you handled that so well." Helena's sarcasm bit hard. Wasn't the boy dealing with enough?

"Mummy, you've no idea how awful it's been," breathed Seraphina as she wriggled her way out of the room.

David pushed open the back door of the cottage. He and Jess had left before the evening party but still, they were longer than they'd intended. Harry was curled up by Sass, who was reading on the couch by the stove. The terrier slipped down and stretched, his tail ticking. Sass put her book down.

"Hey, did you have a good time?"

David made a face and got a prod from Jess.

"Yes, he did" she replied. "They're good friends of ours."

In the space of looking, Sass reminded David of a girl from long ago. Without thinking, he reached for his sketchbook on the side and the pencil that never left his top pocket.

"What are you doing?" Sass asked.

"Sorry, should've checked." David put the pencil down. "Occupational hazard, living with artists."

"Well, then — I guess it's okay." Sass's face glowed, any trace of sickness gone. "No one's wanted to sketch me before.

Better make me look good." She tugged at her hair.

"So how are you after driving off in that Bentley?" Jessie put a hand to Sass's forehead.

"Was that what it was? I never want to go in another one ever again. I was nearly sick on the carpet. Imagine?"

"You've got your colour back at least. I —" Jessie bit her lip. "I didn't know if I should've gone with you, but I know that sometimes — you're happier figuring it out by yourself."

"Honestly, Jessie. I'm fine now."

"So what was she like, the Countess?"

"Who?"

Sass looked up, startled. Her eyes an intense blue.

David drew her quickly: a few light pencil strokes, a dot for a mole, a line for a nose, the curved dark brows and spider eyelashes, and the smudges of sadness still visible below them. He'd seen her once as a baby, almost sixteen years ago. One look at her crying face in his sister's arms before he took off. Now he wanted to protect her. It had crept up on him, this strange but not unwelcome feeling. Not a parent exactly; not a friend either, but someone in between who would take care of things when Sass needed him.

"The Countess of Tremayne. We're restoring her painting." Jess repeated, then demonstrated with a brushstroke and quick curtsy. David snorted. Two bright spots had appeared in Sass's cheeks.

"She called herself Helena. I thought you knew her?"

"Well, yes and no. I mean, she's a client and collects art,

but the Tremaynes are one of Cornwall's most landed families. Different league to us. Her daughter is a princess; you know, lovely clothes, amazing hair, married to the son of the queen, always on the front of Seen magazine."

"Oh. She was just sort of — nice to me. A little uptight and wearing funny clothes for such a hot day."

Sass's face had changed in a few seconds. Taken on a kind of wide-awake quality. David was curious to know why, but glad. She looked more animated than he'd ever seen her. He tuned out of their chatter and reached for Harry's lead. Time for a quiet smoke and a think.

Sass could have danced on water. She looked out of the window at the sinking sun in its indigo sky. A yacht was coming in for the night, its lowered sails billowing and rattling. Where had it come from? And did it matter so much as where it was heading?

After her unexpected and wonderful swim with Alex, she'd let herself in with the key from under the flowerpot, greeted Harry, and then gone and showered, the sand sticking to her in sunburned places. Peeling off her dress, she'd hung it on the back of the bathroom door and caught sight of herself in the mirror. The same girl looked back, only this time flushed and covered in goosebumps, happy with a boy who liked her — who just happened to be a prince.

On her way back from the bathroom, Sass had noticed that the door to David and Jessie's bedroom was ajar. She'd nudged it a little further with her toe. The low ceiling of the light-filled space sloped on two sides to a window that slid up and looked out to sea. It was filled with the heady scent of a sprig of lilac set in a glass jar on the windowsill. Piles of books made makeshift tables beside an unmade bed. Sass looked away, as if she was intruding on their privacy, and was about to back out when a photo in a frame caught her eye. It was an old one, sort of browny black and white. Not much more than a snapshot of a group of soldiers in uniform. The centre guy was lounging in a leather jacket against something she couldn't quite make out, his peaked cap set at an angle and a cigarette dangling from his lips. He was nice-looking. Young. But it was the shape of his face that caught her attention. It was hers. Almost like looking in the misty bathroom mirror. Who was he?

Sass thought of all the pictures in the universe that must exist of Alex and his family. Thousands, maybe? And yet none had registered with her like this one. When did a face in a photo mean something? Did you have to know the person? Or was a face simply what you wanted it to be in your head? She gazed at it again. The man looked so like her that Sass felt she ought to know him. A relative? She had precious few of those. Or was he just some other dead family mystery she knew nothing about? Like her dad. She had no idea who he was, or why he'd never come forward after Mom died. Sass leaned on the sill and tipped her head back to look up at the stars that had come out in the sky, the moon marking the way

157

"to infinity and beyond". Buzz Lightyear, she smiled, her all-time superhero. What would he think was happening to her? Was she flying, or falling with style?

A long way from civilisation, Cressida Slater sat in the dingy bar of The Stragglers, or whatever the dismal place was called. She looked around at the leather-faced locals downing their Saturday-night pints; all she wanted was a little worm for her line. Who was the pretty fish that the prince had gone swimming with today? The little wriggler on camera certainly wasn't Princess Plum, despite the tip-off. Her photographer, Silvio, had done well, but now the new girl needed a name.

She began with a text to Plum, pretending she was still waiting for her news. Miss Benoist messaged straight back.

I changed my mind.

Cressida hid her irritation. Little fool. Her reply, laced with sugar.

Why? We had an agreement, Plum, that you'd talk.

Cressida weighted the line. The hook sharp.

Not about that. The relationship. It's over.

What?

Yes. I finished it.

So soon? What happened? Someone else?

Can't say.

A bite.

Poor u! Who is she? Make it worth your while?

Teasing now.

I saw a name on his hand.

Cressida's heart beat faster — a name

Really?

Yes but never heard of her. Must be a nobody.

Any girl with Prince Alex was somebody.

Tell me.

Cressida wound the fishing line tighter and gave it a sharp tweak.

Sass Chapel.

Cressida switched to email and glanced down at the photos from Silvio uploading on her screen. Oh, these were good! Prince Alex, it seemed, was a two-timer like his father, and leading them all on a merry dance. So not a wasted journey. "You're going global, baby," she whispered to "Sass", the world's newest mystery. All she needed now was some undeniable small proof and a headline. The devil was in the detail. She stuck her tongue out in concentration: "Castles of Sand"? Too romantic. "The Prince and His Little Mermaid"? Too Disney. "The Girl Who Stole a Prince". Just right.

Zooming in, Cressida studied the bony, chestnut-haired girl until she pixelated into a hundred pieces.

26

THE SKETCH

It was Sunday. Amy sat on her morning break with a mug of sweet tea, thinking about yesterday and meeting Plum Benoist. Alex's girlfriend wasn't as ooh-la-la French as her name. Amy blew on her tea. She'd looked amazing arriving in that Porsche, but that's where it ended. She'd had to watch them disappear into the house and take herself off for a bit of a cry. How could she compete with that? It wasn't fair. Later she'd cheered up and gone to the pub, which was where she'd bumped into Dan. The farrier was shoeing the horses behind her now. Came every five weeks without fail, even worked on Sundays. "You and me both," she murmured to herself. Amy could hear the roar of his furnace and the clang of his anvil. The young blacksmith was good. He handled the youngsters gently and kept the older ones sound. Had every stable girl fancying him for miles around. She watched him wrestle a hind shoe off, blond and strong-armed in his vest and leather apron.

Putting her mug down, Amy sank back against the buckets she'd just scrubbed out. One last daydream before she got back to work, no naughtier than chocolate. She closed her eyes, but instead of Dan and a comfy haystack, she was at a polo match smelling gorgeous, her hair all clean and split-end free. She was presenting the trophies and Alex was laughing with his hand on her waist. He'd just leaned over to whisper...

Bang!

The slam of Dan's hammer; and Amy spilled her tea. What was she doing dreaming? It was all pants anyway! She hated what those polo ponies had to put up with. She'd even seen that polo player, the famous one, Eduardo, in the flesh last night when she got back. Not naked; she pulled a face at the thought, though he was ever so tanned with curly black hair. Real too, not fake: his tan, not his hair. He'd flown in with Alex's mother in a helicopter; smiled at her with very white teeth. What was he doing with the princess? She had to be over forty. Amy knew all about Alex's parents. Didn't everyone?

Some nosy reporter had been at the pub last night, offering cash for anything on Alex and someone called Sass. Who? She'd got that all wrong! There was only a Plum and she'd been so tempted to rat on her. It was more money than Amy earned in a week. Not that that made it right. Nobody local would spill about Alex. Not on purpose. The Countess was like legend around here.

After the pub, Dan had given her a lift home in his truck. Told her that life was too short to hang about waiting for a prince. Said it with a rough thumb on her chin like he might want to kiss her. If she wasn't so crazy about Alex, she might have let him.

In the gallery, David was rehanging some new works when the bell on the door tinkled. A customer came in. A thin-faced townie in smart shoes that looked out of place. She'd been standing outside for the last few minutes staring at the sign, "The Chapel Gallery", as if for divine inspiration.

She approached the desk, hardly bothering to glance around. "Excuse me," she said. "Is that your name?"

"Is what my name?"

"Chapel. It's on the sign outside." She looked irritably at him, as if they both knew it was a stupid question.

"Er — no. I'm David Emerson. The gallery is called The Chapel because —" He pointed at the last remaining stained glass window. "It was a chapel. Methodist, I think."

"Ha. The landlord at The Strugglers' End said as much. And do you own this business, Mr Emerson? I mean, is it in your family?"

"My family?"

"Yes. Are you art dealers or connoisseurs or something? Collect old masters, perhaps?"

"Maybe you're mistaking me for someone else? I mean,

if it's a modern seascape you want, I'm your guy. Feel free to look around?"

"Don't mind if I do."

The woman had an inscrutable face. Not the sort he wanted to draw. She obviously read his mind because she glanced down at his sketchbook lying open on the desk. Her sharp eyes glinted slightly and he found himself wanting to cover the drawing of Sass, relieved when the woman took herself off to browse.

She didn't stay away for long.

"Can I see that drawing?" she said pointedly.

"Which drawing?"

"That one under your arm?" She consciously softened her face with a thin smile as if she might forgive him for keeping it from her.

"It's just a sketch; it's not for sale."

"What, a lovely drawing like that? Who is she? She looks so natural. Did you do it?"

"I did. Yes."

"She must be your daughter. What is she, sixteen or seventeen?"

"Sixteen at the end of the month."

"Sweet sixteen. I remember that age."

David couldn't imagine the woman was ever sixteen. Or sweet. Her voice had the gravel of a chain-smoker. Not that he could talk, but he'd stop when everything was sorted.

"That's Saskia, my sister's daughter." He remembered the look on Sass's face last evening and added, "Sass was happier than I've ever seen her. It was a moment to capture."

"Had something wonderful happened?"

"Can't think what." It hadn't occurred to him that anything had. It certainly wasn't the wedding. "She did have a new dress that brought out the blue in her eyes!" He laughed. Sass's recent transformation was hard to pinpoint.

"Ah —"

"But I'm sure you didn't come in here looking for a half-drawn sketch of a smiling teenager?"

"Quite right." Her tone hardened. "What I want is much bigger. Have you any seriously huge — seascapes? These are all quite small." She wafted her hand around the walls.

"How big?"

"The sort you might want to show the world?"

"Err — I have a few. They're mostly bought by collectors, or for corporate use."

"Yes. That's the sort of thing I'm after. Perhaps you've one or two out the back? I don't like to ask, but I'm only passing through, you see?"

"Sure. Won't be a minute. There is one you might like. It's in the storeroom. I'll go get it."

"Don't hurry," she purred. "I'll mind the desk."

27

THE TOWER

Sass closed the door behind her and slipped out into the silvery Monday morning, a small canvas rucksack slung over her shoulder. In her hand she squeezed the key Alex gave her like a talisman. Would the weather hold today? Even this early, the air was as warm as soup. As she crept across the headland, the sun yawned and stretched, then rolled back again behind a dark cloud.

By the time she arrived at the side gate, butterflies were dancing in her stomach. Pulling back the ivy, she took out the key and tried it in the old lock. She expected it to be stiff, but it turned with a surprising click. Shoulder to the door, she heaved it open and stumbled through to a view that made her heart stop; she'd been too engrossed all the times before with scrambling sideways over.

The rolling mist led her eye down to a line of shadowy oaks, bordered by paddocks and the promise of more horses, and at the end rose a great house like a ghost galleon at sea, the faintest ray of sunshine crossing her prow. Sass stood spellbound, Alex's name on her lips as she brushed a damp cobweb from her face. He lived *there*?

Bo's hoofbeats brought her back to the present. The grey mare had cantered up and was shaking her head over a gateway to the meadow. Sass dragged herself away and let herself through, and ran down to the creek to wait.

It wasn't long before Alex arrived. When Bo heard Dancer, she flung up her head and whinnied. Sass looked up too and was rewarded by Alex smiling down at her, sitting tall and straight in the saddle.

"Am I really going to do this again?" she asked, shading her eyes.

"Thought you trusted me after last time? I hope you're ready." His eyes ran over her.

She ignored the flutter in her stomach and tapped her heels together Dorothy-style. "I'm ready!"

"You look..." He dismounted, his shirt riding up. A glimpse of taut skin as he turned and murmured, "Nice."

And with his hands on her waist, it sounded a lot more like beautiful.

It felt strange sitting on Bo in a saddle; much easier than bareback, or last time on Dancer. Better than ten times around on a flying-pink-elephant ride at age six. She had fallen over that time and skinned her knees, giddy with the fun of it. Mom had kissed them. If only she could see her now:

Sass had changed; she'd had to, hadn't she? Not just from being a kid. She was different now in every possible way, the knot in her heart loosening at last, like she could retie it any way she wanted.

Alex was saying something to her about not holding the reins "properly". Sass looked down at him. Stretched her fingers, inches away from his head, and fought an urge to mess with his hair.

"Sass, are you listening?"

"Sorry, no. Tell me again?"

"Like this. Come on, two hands. Thumbs on top. Try to remember."

He frowned slightly and showed her again.

"And when you want to turn, don't forget your legs are more important than your hands." His eyes travelled up to her face and lightened. "But don't worry, you'll be fine."

They wound along a quiet bridle path that rose inland along a wooded creek away from the meadow and the house. Under the trees, everything was muffled by the soft sound of hooves, occasionally brightened by a flash of sunlight through the foliage. Beside them, the creek was flowing fast in the opposite direction, and it seemed as if time was suspended and they weren't moving at all. An hour slowed to the breathing of the horses, the swish of their tails, Alex riding ahead with Bo tucked in behind.

After an age, they reached a clearing where the track sloped upwards. Shoulder to shoulder, the horses sidled in expectation and Sass felt a familiar tremor run through her body when Alex spoke up.

"Look, in a minute, the track opens out. The horses know it, but just sit quietly and try not to tense up. We're only walking, but if they're good and you're feeling ready, we'll have a trot and a gentle canter." He said the word under his breath: Dancer needed no encouragement. Sass could hardly breathe.

He was right. As they turned the bend, a grass track stretched ahead, bordered by a field of wavering silver-white poppies. Dancer was jogging now. His neck had sweated up, foamy where the reins were rubbing. Bo carried on walking, a mother unimpressed by her child playing up.

"I think he'll settle if we trot. Try to find your rhythm: rising up and down like you practised. Hang on to Bo's mane if you need to."

"You just focus on staying on yourself." Sass laughed, because he was the one with his hands full.

They started off well. Sass found the natural rhythm easily and Bo felt calm and even, puffing slightly up the gentle slope. Then just as she was feeling more confident, four deer sprang across their path, so close in front of them that Sass could see their bright, frightened eyes. And that was it. Dancer dropped his shoulder, snorted and bolted, with Bo galloping after him, her hooves sparking on flints.

Sass crouched low over the mare's neck, whispering "Whoa, girl," over and over, more to soothe herself because it made no difference — the horses' blood was up and the two thoroughbreds were flying. Sass's arms shook with the effort of holding on. She had to let go, she had to, but then in the moment that she did, Bo stopped fighting her and somehow she found her balance.

Sass dared to look ahead, only to see a sight that made her quake: a fallen tree lay across the track. Its trunk huge and solid, its waving branches a terrifying warning. Even the wind in her ears shrieked, "Hold up!"

In front, Sass could see Alex sit back and haul with all his strength, but Dancer was a rocket heading for the moon. A fallen tree was nothing to him. Caught off-balance in his wrestle with his rider, he jumped cat-like, his head in the air, and cleared it with ease.

Too soon, it was Bo's turn, for the mare was taking her there. The horse had steadied to a pulse-pounding canter, her eyes locked on the jump to come, and Sass waited, forever, for the inevitable leap. At last, she felt Bo gather herself up, her hind legs strong beneath her, and then ... And then, they were soaring into the sky in a moment of heart-stopping suspension, an arc of perfect madness.

As Bo's front feet touched down, Sass sat back, her feet braced against the stirrups. Oh my god, they'd made it, and she'd never felt so alive.

Alex couldn't believe what had just happened. Sass hadn't fallen. He'd managed to stop Dancer at the summit of the hill and wasn't sure who was breathing harder, him or the horse.

He watched Sass canter up behind him sitting remarkably straight; only her hands clutched in Bo's mane gave her away.

"God, are you O.K.?" He reached out and caught her wrist. "Dancer just took off."

"Don't think you'll do that again —" she said, grinning from ear to ear "— gallop off and leave me standing."

Relief flooded through him.

"You're amazing, you know?"

Sass wrinkled her nose. "Seriously?"

"Really, truly, incredibly. I can't seem to ditch you!"

"Better stick with me, then..."

"Don't worry. I intend to."

Alex straightened up, sure in his own mind.

"Where are we heading?"

"Somewhere I think you'll like." He looked up at the sky. "I'm just hoping the weather will hold." The clouds were hunkering down.

"Where?"

"You'll see; it's not far from here."

There was only one other place where Alex knew they could be alone, from a time in the past when secrets were guarded by knights and paid for with lives.

They rode further inland, climbing a steep-sided ridge that cradled the estate in the crook of its arm. Turning in the saddle, Sass could see for miles around, and not just the way that they'd come. She could see the ocean and even the coast path stretching past the beach and on to the village. Sass patted Bo's neck, the mare's long mane lifting in the shifting wind; they weren't far now from the top of the rise.

At a cluster of wind-blown trees, Alex reined in and dismounted. Sass slid off too, clutching the saddle as her knees buckled.

"I'm going to ache tomorrow."

"Stop complaining and come here."

She went over to him, leading Bo. Alex left Dancer to graze, tucking his reins behind his stirrups, and did the same with Bo. Stepping behind Sass, he put his hands over her eyes.

"Keep walking until I say you can open them."

She must have taken about twenty stumbling steps.

"Okay, now you can."

She was standing in front of a tower, a ruin really, fallen to pieces and overgrown with flowering brambles.

"It's twelfth century — what's left of a castle keep. Not that there's much left to see. Too many storms."

Sass gazed about her, shivering slightly. This wasn't some movie set, but real. Bows and arrows. Kings and queens. Blood and battle.

Alex grabbed her by the hand and led her towards the entrance to a last remaining stone turret.

"Come in here. It's a cracking view. You can see three hundred and sixty degrees from the top."

Hand in hand, they stepped inside. The tread of their boots echoed slightly and Sass's hand trailed across a bulging stone wall. The smell was damp and salty as seaweed.

"Be careful. The floor, and especially the steps, are uneven, and at the top it just falls away where the ramparts have crumbled in the sea air."

"Is it safe? I'm not a fan of heights."

"I very much doubt it," Alex grinned, "but it's stood this long and I want to show you."

He let her go first up the circular stairwell, his hands on her hips as if to catch her if she fell. She stepped up through the darkness with her heart in her mouth, one step at a time towards the light, to emerge mole-like and blinking.

"Oh, wow!" She clung to the edge and gazed at the view.

"Watch your step. Here, hold my hand."

The drop seemed to plunge away to the coast path below, and below that, the sea crashed on the rocks.

Alex pointed past her ear. Sass wanted him to hang on to her hand again, but instead his fingers slid down her arm, and past her ribs to her waist. She'd never noticed her ribs before and for a second, Sass felt a giggle rise up in her. Giddy, dizzy, light-headed with it all, as if she might step out and float.

"To the left of you is Trist. Look, down there in the valley and ahead of you is the English Channel."

Sass thought that the gleaming rooftops of Trist looked like some Celtic crown against a tapestry of green that ended at a shield of sea.

"Behind us, not so many miles away, is Tintagel, birthplace of King Arthur."

She shivered. "The once and future king. I thought he was a myth?"

"All legend is based on some sort of truth."

"So you're not the first royal to duck out of sight in Cornwall?"

"No! There's always been something going on in my history. It's how we got to where we are."

"Maybe your ancestors just got away with more?"

He kissed her ear. "No. They got imprisoned, or beheaded or died horribly in battle, which is unlikely to happen to me."

"So all this land is part of Trist?"

"Yes. Took a few hundred years. Wars. Marriages. Deaths. And, I imagine, a good bit of luck and family in high places."

High places meant skyscrapers to Sass, and she hadn't had any luck with family. No history peeking through paint cracks for her. Would she ever tell him about Mom? Soon, but not now: not while she was on top of the world. She couldn't even begin to think about the rest of Alex's legacy. It just made her dizzier. Anyway, she didn't have to, not right now, did she? It was like hearing about black holes; the theory of a universe that she ought to be interested in, but that scared her. Who wanted to be reminded that they weren't so much as a speck of dust?

Sass turned into Alex's arms and the hardness of his body. He lifted her on her toes and when they kissed, it was long and slow, until she lost herself in his touch.

"Shall I tell you the story of Tristan and Iseult?" Alex's nose touched her ear lobe.

"Tell me," she replied, listening for the soft tread of a slipper and the rustle of a gown.

"Tristan was the nephew of King Mark of Cornwall."

She lifted her face.

"Was he handsome?"

"Tristan? Yes, very. He was a young knight sent to Ireland because his uncle, King Mark, wanted to marry a beautiful Irish princess called Iseult."

"Why are they always beautiful?" Sass sighed.

"Err — Because she's a princess — in a legend."

"I bet she was blonde, or a redhead. They're always red-headed, the fiery ones."

"You'd rather she had hair like yours?" Alex reached forward and tucked a strand stuck to her lip, behind her ears.

"Yeah, why not?"

"Just for you, then. They called her — Frizzy Izzie."

Sass grinned and let his voice sink in.

"Tristan was sent to Ireland to pay tribute by facing his uncle's rival in combat. He defeated the man, but was injured by a poisoned arrow."

"Don't tell me, Izzie healed his wounds?"

"She did, and they fell for each other."

Sass smiled and closed her eyes, feeling Alex draw breath.

"They couldn't run, so they returned to Cornwall. Both knew their duty." He paused on the last word.

"King Mark of course wanted to marry Iseult. And he did. At first, Tristan tried to stay away, but he couldn't because he loved her too much. They met in secret, in a tower like this — until his uncle found out. There are always spies. King Mark could have put them both to death, but he didn't; he let them live, banishing Tristan forever."

Sass gulped. "And?"

"They lived out their separate lives till, on his deathbed , Tristan sent a boat for Iseult. He'd married too, but had never forgotten his first love. He asked for the sails to be white if she came, black if she didn't. But Tristan's wife found out — and it all went wrong. Tristan and Iseult died of broken hearts."

Sass curled inward. Everything came down to what was black and white when nothing ever was.

"That's so sad."

"Not entirely. Legend has it that a hazel and a honeysuckle grew on their grave and became so entwined, they could never be cut down."

A large blob of rain landed between them.

"Come on," said Alex, looking at the sky. "We should check on the horses."

They climbed back down to where Bo and Dancer were still happily grazing and leaving them a while longer, sat down in the shelter of the wall. Sass shrugged off her rucksack.

"I've brought you something," she said.

She had almost forgotten.

"You have? What is it?" Alex looked surprised but pleased

"It's nothing, just something to eat. Are you hungry? I made it myself." Pride in her voice. She and Mom hadn't got that far with cooking.

Sass took out a small tub. Taking off the lid, she held it out.

"Brownies. From me to you, to say thanks."

"Whatever for?"

"For —" she waved a hand around her — "for all this — for being my knight. I don't know. Just — thanks."

Alex took a piece from her, careful not to drop it or let it crumble. He took a bite and couldn't speak, his mouth was so full. Broke a chunk off and shared it with her. It was warm and gooey, and it tasted good.

"You've missed a bit," he said. Her tongue went to the corner of her mouth, but his thumb got there first and wiped the smear softly from her lip.

"I think your American brownie just won." He caught her eye, and looking back at him Sass knew she'd see chocolate sweet-swirling in her sleep. It was a moment when they could have said or done anything. Told each other everything.

A rumble of thunder split the sky. The weather had broken, shaken from its daze. Dancer threw up his head and snorted down his nose, and Alex jumped up to catch him.

"We'd better get going. It can be foul up here, and they'll only wonder where I am."

Sass dashed the crumbs from her lap and took his hand.

"Another time…" He whispered, as he handed her Bo's reins.

The rain came down as they rode. It swept in across the steep hillside and the horses turned their backs to it. Dancer crabbed sideways, and even Bo skidded and slipped. Alex kept trying to shout advice, but Sass couldn't hear him any more, unaware even he was taking her a different way back.

Alex had come to a decision. Rather than stopping at the meadow to leave Bo, they'd go back an easier route and ride on to the house. It would be safer than this. The squall would have made the way they'd come too slippery in the wet, and Dancer, even with Bo by his side, would lose it if lightning struck. They'd follow the curve of the ridge until it sloped down to the village road. It was the longer way home and they'd come in the front, but perhaps that was right, given what Grandma, and his parents, were about to find out. He owed it to Sass to tell them about her. She deserved to know what she meant to him. He couldn't say the words, but he felt them, and even if he'd shouted, "*I love you!*" a thousand times, the wind and rain would still have ripped them away before she heard them. Wet to the skin, Sass's clothes hugged her body, while Bo ploughed on, oblivious to Dancer skating beside her.

They reached the main road, where Alex looked left and right, before striking out on the tarmac. It was only a hundred or so yards to the front gates around the corner.

Heads down against the rain, they came out of the bend, and Dancer saw them first. He planted his feet and baulked, spinning around with his head in the air, and Alex only just held him.

Cameras.

It took a while for the huddle of TV vans and reporters to realise who was coming up behind them, but the clatter of wet hooves was too loud not to draw attention.

"It's *him*," came the collective clamour. The words he hated most, and suddenly they were all around like hounds at a kill. Dancer was up on his haunches cantering sideways and Sass looked bewilderedly across at him, hanging on to an agitated Bo. Alex reached across and took her reins, struggling to keep control of his own. Grateful for Bo's steadier bulk, Dancer glued himself to the older horse, and together Alex and Sass were able to kick on, Alex acutely aware they were adding to the drama unfolding. What had his parents done now? He gritted his teeth, rougher with Dancer than usual.

"Get on with it!" he hissed to the horse with a sharp slap to his neck with the reins.

What were cameras doing here in Cornwall?

The answer came next.

"Sir, sir. Is she the one? The girl on the beach?" "What?"

"How did you meet Saskia, Your Highness? Did you meet her here, or in the States?"

"How the...?" Dumbfounded again.

The pack turned on Sass with quick-fire questions that she couldn't possibly answer.

"Is it true, Saskia, that you're 'happier' with the prince 'than ever before'?"

"What's your reaction to those pictures from the beach?" "Where's the dress from, the one you bought specially?" And the best saved for last.

"What was it that first drew you to the prince: his good looks, his position, or his horses?"

Sass gaped like a fish. A floundering, flapping, wet fish. "I — I — What are you talking about?"

Alex thought she might fall. Questions elbowed and jostled in his own mind about what the press knew. He wheeled around and, reins in one hand, leaned out of the saddle and shoved away a long lens from Bo's face. Then he pressed Dancer forward and sideways, stroking the horse's neck, physically blocking Sass from any more intrusion, his foot rammed in the front of a TV camera.

"Sass, kick on. Just go! I'm right behind you." Dancer spun wildly as Bo pulled away, but Alex held his ground.

They made it back to the yard in a sorry spray of mud and water. Figgy looked up first, strode across, hands on hips. A ship in full sail.

"Alex! Where in god's name have you been? Your grandmother's waiting!" Figgy thrust a crumpled newspaper in his hand. "You didn't say where you were going, or for how long, and — what on earth are you doing with Bo? She's not fit. Look at the state of her."

Figgy glanced up at Sass and her eyes narrowed as if to say, "Who's she?" but she stopped herself in time.

Alex dismounted, his boots squelching as he landed. His voice had gone. Nothing left to say. Amy appeared from the feed room, her eyes popping out of her head. With a sharp nod from Figgy, she took Dancer from him, still staring at Sass, who had slid awkwardly to the ground. Bo waited with her head lowered, steam rising from her wet coat.

Alex ran up Bo's stirrups and took off her old saddle. He walked the mare to her stable with Sass stumbling behind. The only sound was the plink of water running off a gutter.

"This isn't what I wanted." He was shaking.

"That's okay," Sass whispered, avoiding the obvious question. "You didn't make it rain."

She looked away, twisting her hair. Was she playing dumb? How could the papers have possibly known all that — unless she told them? Her name, where she came from. He shook out the paper.

The girl he thought he could trust. The girl he'd been ready to love.

Pressure built in his head until he thought he'd explode.

28

BETRAYED

In the stable, the downpour slowed to a patter on the roof. Sass glanced at Alex, who refused to meet her eyes.

"What are you thinking?" she asked, a hesitant hand on his arm.

"Nothing." He shrugged her off.

"Yes, you are! I can tell. You haven't said a word since we met those reporters."

"I was thinking —" his voice icier than she'd ever heard it — "that I was going to introduce you to my grandmother because I thought it was important. Now it seems I don't need to."

Sass froze at his words. "Why? What do you mean it's not important?"

"I mean that the press will have told her everything already and more — Saskia Emerson? You heard them at the gates." His words were tinged with the sarcasm that she thought she'd forgotten, from that first time they met. He

181

thrust a newspaper at her, which she fumbled, and watched as it fell to the ground in a scatter of wet pages

Was that a photo of her? Sass knelt down. The front page lay face up and must have been taken from high up on the cliff top. Not that it mattered because the camera had zoomed in so close. She was standing on the beach with her back to the lens, holding hands with Alex in his shorts, her dress gaping open in the breeze for all to see. She could trace her spine all the way to her waist. Her face grew hot. "It wasn't like that," she whispered in her head. She turned to the headline, feeling sick already, and got sicker. Sick to her churning stomach.

THE GIRL WHO STOLE A PRINCE

Cressida Slater reporting for the Daily Sun

Our handsome sixteen-year-old prince has been consoling himself after his parents' split, not in the arms of his "devastated" English girlfriend, blonde heiress Plum Benoist, who visited him this weekend, but on a beach in Cornwall with a scantily clad American, who cast aside a new dress to frolic half naked in the waves. The Daily Sun can exclusively reveal that the long-limbed lovely is mystery mermaid Saskia Emerson, who a source reports is "happier than ever before". Since playing truant from his prestigious public school, the rebel prince has so far spent the summer unwinding at his grandmother's country estate: riding, swimming ... and, it seems, fishing.

Like father, like son? Young love, or love rat? Have your say. Follow #palacealex.

How could they possibly know so much, let alone twist it all like that? Made more real in black and white: her name, her head, her body, her thoughts. And – Sass flinched – Plum Benoist, the girl she'd read about in that magazine in the salon. Had she visited Alex here? He'd never said a word.

Alex stood tall before her. Tall, straight and unreadable. He glanced away.

"I didn't speak to anyone, Alex! You do believe me?"

"Then how does the press know so much, Sass, if you didn't tell them? Where you're from, how you felt. More than you've even told me!"

He spat the word "felt". Past tense. That wasn't right.

"It is how I feel..." Sass quivered. "But I'm not the one who told them!" She felt the anger boil up inside her; how dare he accuse her! This boy who all this time still had kept an English girlfriend!

Alex was looking at her with something like pity. She didn't want his pity! What did she want? Honesty, maybe? Though that seemed impossible, given who he was. She strangled a sob. When it was just the two of them together, everything was easy, and the rest just kind of melted away.

"You don't understand," He said. The fire in his eyes burned her. "In my world, secrets are important. They're like the best and the worst, but the more they mean to me, to you, to us, the more we risk. We find each other, but the world sees an opportunity. You can never tell the press anything because stuff will get twisted that can't be controlled."

He kicked at a pile of straw and Bo swung around, afraid.

A little voice cried out in Sass's head that wouldn't be quiet. "Stuff happens anyway, Alex! You can't control it any more than you can hold back the tide."

She should know.

Alex took her by the hand, roughly now, and they left the stable. His fingers tight around hers, almost tugging her through the dripping archway. As they came out, she gazed up at Trist House, close enough to touch, the place she'd glimpsed from a distance. The house was huge, beautiful and disapproving, and Sass's head swam with the scent of wet lavender and roses.

From the corner of her eye, something else added to her confusion: David's battered green Land Rover was parked outside with a familiar black doggy face at the window and then from inside the front entrance came a pronounced, raised voice that she half recognized. The old lady from the church. Alex's grandmother. The Countess, of course! This was her home and she, Saskia Laura Emerson, had not been invited.

"Ah! So there you are at last!"

If the old lady was shocked to see her grandson standing on her porch holding hands with a soaking-wet girl she'd last seen dry-heaving, she didn't show it. Not a flicker. Behind her stood David. Sass wriggled her hand free. What was her uncle doing there? Oh god, could it get any worse? Her uncle was staring at Alex. The Countess was the first to speak again, her voice clipped.

"I see that a few introductions are in order."

Her gaze would have frozen oceans. "We've just been discussing you both."

A pause on the plural that lasted too long.

"Mr Emerson, this is my grandson, Alexander, only son of my daughter, Princess Seraphina."

Sass watched her uncle shake Alex's automatic, outstretched hand while both stood rooted to the ground.

David hadn't believed it until he saw Sass with his own eyes, holding hands with the boy he'd seen on TV! That woman at the gallery had been a snooping journalist from the Daily Sun. Like a fool, he'd told her about Sass: suckered in by her praise of his art. How she'd worked out the rest, he'd no idea.

When the Countess's butler had summoned him an hour ago, he'd locked up the gallery and come. The Countess had been kind to Sass at the wedding. He doubted she'd feel the same way now, but he had to try to explain, if only for Sass's sake.

He'd wrapped the restored painting of the horses in oilskin and put it in the back of the Land Rover, before rattling up the long mile or so to Trist with Harry sitting beside him on top of the incriminating newspaper.

David had parked and taken his time, not sure what he was letting himself in for. The front door was open but he pulled the bellrope anyway, hearing the distant jangle deep inside the house. In the hallway he could see a bronze sculpture of a horse lying on a polished round table. An Elisabeth Frink. The weather-beaten creature was lying down, asleep, its eyes closed to the elements. It looked so vulnerable that he couldn't help but go in and touch it.

"Isn't she beautiful?"

He jumped. He'd been expecting a butler to come to the door, not the Countess herself.

"Every morning," she continued, "I stroke her head for luck. If you look closely, you'll see the tiniest shiny patch between her ears. Stuff and nonsense, of course, especially during current circumstances, but rather comforting, don't you think?"

An hour later, standing beside her errant grandson, Helena fixed her piercing stare on the uncle and niece. There was an obvious family likeness: the blue of their eyes and the shape of their mouths. When she'd first seen Saskia's uncle bent over her sculpture, she'd thought of someone else. A ghost from the war. Silly her. She'd given herself a hard pinch because it was only the faintest resemblance. The past playing tricks on her.

Helena knew of David Emerson by trade because she'd chosen him to restore her beloved foam horses. Saskia had mentioned the family connection when they'd driven back from the church. A well-intended conversation with a grieving girl had taken on a whole new and rather shocking significance. She and Alex were clearly ... attached. She'd pieced that much together from that ghastly rag of a paper and the girl's accent, of course. If only she'd listened to Alex properly during that briefest of conversations over dinner about meeting a friend with Bo, all this unpleasantness might have been avoided. She sniffed. Alex had blatantly disobeyed her.

The uncle's accent was curious: a hint of transatlantic drawl, although everyone sounded American these days. If she closed her eyes, it really could be him. Her lost airman from the war. She lingered on the recollection, reluctant to let it go. He was so often on her mind these days.

Helena had shown David to the quiet of the drawing room so they could discuss what to do, but her gaze had swept past him and the faded silk curtains; beyond the rain-splattered glass of the French windows, where a spider hung by a thread; all the way down the lavender lawn of her memory to where an American boy in uniform had once stood and waited for her.

She inhaled the scent of it now and it calmed her. No wonder the girl had fallen for her grandson. Trist was a place to fall in love. Poor Saskia deserved a little happiness, but how could she find it with this family? Wasn't it her responsibility, as Alex's other grandmother, to steer him toward someone, well, more suitable? More robust. A girl, to put it bluntly, less damaged.

Sass felt like screaming. Everyone was respectfully ignoring each other. The longest silence dripped between them. Drip. Drip. Drip. Sass willed Alex to catch her eye, but he didn't. He didn't even try, instead he went up and down on his toes as if on the edge of exploding. Why would he not look at her? She couldn't hold it in any longer.

"Look at me, Alex? Talk to me!" She held her hands wide, but he clenched his jaw and looked away, fists bunched by his sides, and when he eventually, turned to her ashen-faced, she saw that the fire in his eyes had gone.

In her sodden jeans pocket, the key to the meadow felt suddenly cool. Ice cold. Sass had liked Alex so much; was a little in love with him. She'd kept their secret, just as she'd promised, but this ... *this*, and the awfulness of seeing herself in print, was just too much. She ran down the steps leaving a trail of wet straw. Taking out the key, she flung it away, covering her ears with her hands to muffle the sound of her heart breaking. She had to get away. To think. To find Harry, that small naughty dog who came to her rescue every time she could no longer rely on people.

29

SOME SAD GIRL

Sass heard the knock on the boat-shed loft door, but ignored it. She just wanted to be on her own. She'd stepped out of her puddling wet clothes and put on old pyjamas: brushed pink cotton with baby owls on, bought when she was twelve. It didn't matter now that they didn't reach much past her knees. Nothing mattered.

The weight on her chest was back. Her one consolation: that Mom would never know how stupid she'd been.

The knock came again. "Sass, can I come in?"

Every cell in her body shouted "no". But Jessie didn't wait for an answer. She lifted the latch and walked right in, before sitting down at the end of the bed.

"Oh, Sass — talk to me?"

"Why? I got it all wrong, that's all."

"What did you get wrong, my love?"

"That he liked me, believed me."

"You mean ... um, Prince Alex?"

Like Jessie couldn't believe it herself.

"Yes, Alex!" Just a stupid boy, not god almighty.

"Aren't you being too hard on yourself?" Jessie frowned. "He didn't pressure you into anything, did he?"

Jessie was thinking of the photo, of course. Sass cringed and buried her face.

"No! Not like that." Muffled voice. "I thought it would work out between us, even after I knew who he was. I didn't think of what came with it, or what might happen next. I didn't think. End of."

"Did he lie to you, then?"

"Yes — and no. He was always so secretive. He wanted us to be a secret. He didn't want the world to find out, or maybe — maybe it was because he didn't think I was good enough? Or because he had a girlfriend already. I'd have believed anything because it felt so good; it felt special."

"Oh, sweetheart, I'm so sorry. Did you tell him about you?"

"No. I never did." Sass swallowed. "At first I didn't know him well enough and then later, I didn't want to ruin things. Some sad girl crying for her mom. I just wanted to be normal again. I just wanted to feel — wanted."

Jessie took both her hands. "You are normal and you are wanted, just dealing with some big stuff."

A swell rose inside Sass like the sea below her window.

"I would've scared him off. We might never have come this far."

"How far's that?" Jessie looked anxious again.

"Far enough to think — I could breathe."

And the swell became a wave that broke on the shore while Jessie held her. Some sad girl, crying for a mom she no longer had, over a boy she never would.

30

THE DECISION

Alex had watched Sass go, numb from head to foot. He'd picked up the key and the crumpled paper and slumped in the corner of Dancer's stable. Shutting his eyes, he concentrated on the steady munch of his horse. He looked down at the front page, the thing he loathed most: being Public Property Number One. People talking, tweeting, smirking.

Sass had blabbed to the press. He still couldn't believe it! And would never forgive her. Grinding the heels of his hands in his face, he crushed the Gollum inside him, whining for what he couldn't have. She'd gone. He'd lost her finally. The Land Rover lurching off worse than a kick in the guts.

How stupendously ironic that the one girl – the only girl – he thought had liked him for being him instead of for what he was, had made him look like a fool. She'd kissed him and then betrayed him the very next day. At best, she'd been naïve. He couldn't blame her for the photograph. *His* fault.

He should have known better than to be seen in public, but then, she was the one who'd followed him to the beach that day. Must have told that journalist, that cow, Cressida Slater of all people. Some things, private things, weren't for sharing. He heard the voice of his father: never wear your private life on your public sleeve. Drummed into him since birth. He reached a hand up to Dancer, who nudged him with his nose. If this was "falling for" someone, he'd fallen flat on his arse. What was the point of figuring it out any more? His life was one epic fail.

Helena thought that she'd seen everything – she wasn't that short-sighted yet – however, she was shocked that Alex was so swift to disbelieve the girl. He'd stood there stiff as a soldier. Helena closed her eyes and felt her heart contract. Should she have said or done something? So often these days, her heart missed a beat, or drummed a little out of time.

Helena thought of Saskia bent double in the churchyard, pale as a ghost, trying to be brave in the face of her loss. Was falling in love with her grandson so wrong? They were young. They loved horses and being together. Wasn't that enough? It should be. Why should the rest matter?

Well, it did. She pursed her lips. Alex lived his life in a goldfish bowl; it was the price of privilege. He knew the rules and he'd flouted them, and now both would pay the price. She shook her head. That photograph on the beach; the unfastened back of Saskia's dress blowing in the breeze. It was hardly in flagrante delicto, "caught in the act", but they were both very young, and it was undoubtedly true that it would be for the best, and certainly easier, if they broke up now. Life was perilous enough; a bridle path of twisted tree roots. She knew. It had happened to her all those years ago, during a war that had been the making and breaking of her. Helena's heart gave a little leap; it still hurt after all this time.

She found Alex down in Dancer's stable and put her hand on his head, his hair so unruly in the damp.

"Alex, won't you come inside?"

"No. Just leave me alone," he said through gritted teeth.

"I'm so sorry, darling."

"It's not your fault. It's mine. And now it's over and that's good, isn't it?"

His tone shocked her, if not the sentiment.

"Well, it does need thinking about."

"Honestly, Grandma, just leave it!"

She paused and took a breath.

"You mean, what could I possibly know or understand? You'd be surprised, dear boy. Now come inside and let's talk."

Alex got to his feet. He followed his grandmother into the kitchen and watched as she sat down at the head of the table. In the old Windsor chair, she seemed suddenly small. His gran, getting older. She clasped her hands on the century-old table. He took in the fat, arthritic knuckles, clumsy fingers now, that had once handled reins with the lightest of touches. Hands that had dusted him off every time he fell over, or fell off, or fell for a girl he couldn't stop thinking about.

"Look, I want you to believe in Saskia, but it's better that it ends here," she told him, lips pressed tight.

"Well, I don't believe in her any more. And I doubt she wants me either."

"Listen, Alexander. This isn't about you, or the mistakes you've made — in being together. Saskia should never, ever have to deal with anything like this again. Such exposure is dreadful." She glowered at the paper in his hand and something inside him flared.

Why was his grandmother taking *her* side?

"What are you saying?" So unfair. His feelings mattered too, didn't they? He was the one betrayed.

"How well do you know her? Saskia, I mean?"

"Not as well as I thought."

"I met her once before today." His grandmother's chin trembled.

"What? You didn't think to mention it at the time?" He spat out the words, not caring if he was rude.

"How was I to know of your — relationship? I met her quite by chance in the churchyard the day before yesterday — when your mother came to stay. I rather doubt she knew who I was."

"Oh. . ."

"What if I told you. . ." His grandmother's voice dropped. "That this isn't the moment to be thinking about yourself, your own hurt pride, or that the world is against you. Life is good and your life is the best. This girl, Saskia, hasn't had it easy. She doesn't need any more heartache."

"Why? What are you talking about? How do you know?"

"It's not for me to say." Grandma was firm. She stood up stiffly. "I think perhaps it's time for a drink, something stronger. Medicinal. Won't you join me in the study?"

His grandmother poured them each a tot of his great-grandfather's last remaining single-malt Scotch whisky.

"Down the hatch," she said.

Alex stared at the swirling amber; he hated the stuff and wouldn't drink it. On his father's side he knew his lineage by heart. All the way back to the Magna Carta. On his mother's side, he knew far less and had never met his grandfather, who was already old when Grandma had married him. As for his great-grandfather, the earl had shot himself in the woods a few years after he returned from the First World War. His young daughter, Helena, was not enough to live for when so many others had died. This was his smoking room. His brown boots still stood to attention in the corner. He looked up now and the old stag's head on the wall looked back, and in that dead creature's face, he realised there was only one way out of this mess. One way he could protect Sass from what came next, because he knew how the press would twist it. What they might turn up later.

He'd leave. Go back to London, as far away as possible. He'd be the fox for the hounds. He'd do his parents' fake photos, smile dutifully for the cameras, do whatever they wanted, so long as the press stopped wanting more of her. He picked up the smoky drink and chucked it in the fireplace. Gazing down at Sass's head in the photo he'd kept in his pocket, he ran his thumb lightly down her spine before crushing the newspaper into a ball and reaching for the matches.

Turning back to his grandmother, he searched the lines of her face.

"You didn't say if you liked her?"

Helena thought of the lonely girl in her flower-print dress at the churchyard. The sort of teadress that she'd worn once. She remembered Sass's tearful revelation and the way the girl had carried herself that day. She had wiped her face and put her shoulders back, and shown ... true grit. She was a girl to admire.

But Saskia Emerson had been through the mill. Helena watched the creased edges of the paper catch light, bit back the truth and looked up.

"I liked her immensely, darling, but really, is she quite right for you?"

Her grandson looked away, and there wasn't a more unhappy boy in all of England, Scotland, Northern Ireland and Wales.

Alex had spent a restless and lonely night on the rooftop. After the head spin of the day before, doubts crowded in. Could he have been wrong about Sass? Was there another explanation?

How could he know for sure if he didn't go and find her? Even Grandma knew more than he did. But what had he missed? And why hadn't Sass told him?

He crouched with his back to the wall, the wind lashing the distance between them. He imagined her asleep, her hair across her face. Did she sleep on her front, or back, or curled up on her side? Had she told him the truth? Was she tricked? Was she bribed? It happened all the time. Alex picked up a broken shard of slate and scratched her initials in the stone between his feet.

As dawn broke, the cockroach was back, his father's staff Range Rover came crawling up the drive with its darkened windows. It was 6 a.m. Last evening, both of his parents had rung on the landline from different places, united in their separate outrage. Corbett had put them through. His mother had been shrill, fussing about police protection 24-7, while his father seemed oddly surprised at his son's decision to return so soon.

Alex dressed quickly. Whatever the truth, leaving was the right thing to do, before he caused more trouble for any of them. But no way could he go without seeing Sass one last time.

He slipped down the old servants' staircase. Through the kitchen door, he could hear the foghorn voice of Fellowes. Poor Mr and Mrs C, their morning tea ruined. Alex edged his way past and was almost out of the back door when he smacked into a younger, bald-headed guy having a quiet smoke by the basement steps. A newbie. Royal Protection. Alex had never seen him before, and he was blocking the way.

The policeman dropped his cigarette, stubbing it out with a steel toecap. He stepped forward with his hand out. Alex shook it. Wary. The man had a grip like a boxer and a face to match.

"Sir, I'm Inspector James Harrison."

"Alexander," Alex replied, "You're very early." Pressure in his chest.

"Sorry about that. Palace orders."

"I see. How long have I got to get ready?" Feigning indifference: struggling inside.

How would he get past him?

"Soon as you're ready, sir. Press are gathering at the gates."

"More press?" Alex choked back his dismay. "And Miss Emerson, have we sent police around to her?"

Wherever Sass was staying in the village, there'd be reporters camped nearby. The new policeman looked at him. His gaze was firm. Unbending. This was his job and he didn't intend to lose it like his predecessor.

"I expect so, sir, but I suggest you pack. I'm here if you need me."

Alex shook his head, twitchy as if someone were flicking his brain.

"I have to do something first."

"That depends..." said his policeman steadily.

"It's private." Spoken too quickly.

"I think you know, sir, the importance of listening to orders."

"Well..." Alex spluttered, hot under the collar. "I'm telling you, there's something I still have to do. I have to see someone — a girl." No point in pretending. He appealed to the man behind the suit. Not happening. He might have been a prince, but it seemed he didn't make the rules.

"I'm sorry, sir. It's like I said. Soon as you're ready. We have to be gone by —" the man looked at his watch — "seven o'clock."

Fifteen minutes.

Alex was screwed. It wasn't a question of try harder; there'd be a detailed route, secured from A to Z, with every letter covered in between in case, one day, his life depended on it.

Think! He felt the weight of the key in his pocket and turned it between his fingers. Drawing out his hand, palm up, he saw the faded ink stain. Had he time to write her a note? "See it as romantic," she'd murmured, right after he kissed her the first time. He'd write her a note now, if she wanted to read it...

"Look, inspector, I've left something undone, something important — on the yard."

"No messing?" The policeman scrutinised him but his face creased kindly. "Be quick, then."

"Thank you."

"That's all right, sir. And it's Jim."

Alex legged it down to the tack room. Inside, he scrabbled around for a pen and paper, found the stump of a pencil and an old hay invoice. Hardly romantic. What did you say to the girl you'd lied to, then kissed time and again, and then blamed for something that may not have been her making? He started scribbling, pressing so hard that he went through the paper. Three words he needed to say.

Alex looked up when he finished. Now all he had to do was get it to her. His eyes lit on Amy brushing Bo on the yard in the hazy sunshine. He'd ask her to take it to Sass at her uncle's gallery. She'd do it, of course. He and Amy had been friends for a long time.

Less than ten minutes later, Alex slumped in the back of the car, hidden behind its blacked-out windows as the muddled green lanes from Trist became B roads, then A roads that straightened out into motorways. Six long hours back to London.

31

A CRAB BENEATH A ROCK

The Range Rover accelerated smoothly through the golden gates of Kensington Palace, past the crowds of tourists and the rest. As they drew up to the great house, Alex saw his father waiting in person. Unusual. He even stepped forward to open the car door, his face lined and drawn.

"Good to see you, Alex." He didn't sound happy.

"You too — I —" Alex was lost for words; his father was often stern, but rarely miserable.

"No need to say anything now. Let's get you inside." He turned to Jim, who stood respectfully back.

"Thank you, inspector."

Jim nodded.

Fellowes went to follow, but his father put up his hand with a faint frown.

"I'll take it from here. Thank you for bringing him back in one piece."

They walked up to the apartment. Even in this green part of London, Alex felt the cage of the city close around him. The belch of traffic, the thump of building works, the whoop of a siren. Even the water in the fountain went around in an endless circuit.

He was a monkey in a zoo.

Only when he shrugged off his rucksack did he begin to relax. His father's butler, Barrow, took the half-empty bag without a raised eyebrow. Alex often wondered what he really thought of the family he worked for.

With puffy, bloodshot eyes, his father looked exhausted. *Here we go.* Alex expected a cold blast of disapproval, but instead his father reached out and put a hand briefly on his son's shoulder.

"I'm glad you're here. This hasn't been easy for you — for any of us. The talk of a divorce is giving the press a field day and I'm afraid you're rather caught up in the whole sorry affair." He murmured the last word, hung his head and grimaced to keep his composure.

Weirdly, Alex felt himself sag like he'd been holding up something huge. He slumped against his father. The relief at resting his aching head and breathing in cigar smoke and cologne. A million miles from a girl with tangled hair who tasted of chocolate and rain.

Sass lay curled in bed. A crab beneath a rock. As the midday Tuesday sun snuck around, she stuck her head out from under her pillow. On the floor beside her was yesterday's Daily Sun.

Jessie had come up earlier with a cup of tea and the excuse of taking Harry out, but Sass had burrowed deeper, blocking out the world. Seabirds squabbled and screeched. Boats rattled. Dogs barked. Life went on without her, everything the same, as if nothing had changed. Nothing. She hugged the untruth of that like a cramp in her stomach.

Sometime later, when the watery sunlight began to dip, crabgirl stirred. She rolled onto her stomach, put her hand down to the floor and slid it over the front page.

Alex was holding her hand in the photo, a split-second moment captured in a click. She had just touched his hair, tousled from the salt. She remembered that his eyes had been so dark, and earnest. They'd been good together, hadn't they? So why hadn't he believed her? She'd never have told.

Sass sat up and wrenched a strip off the newsprint. Followed it with another frustrated tear, and then a sharper rip. One piece at a time, paper petals of heartache.

"He loves me.

"He loves me not.

"He loves me."

So many times that she soon lost count, until the last one, which floated to the floor in a draft from the open window.

"He loves me not."

Sass looked in dismay at the pieces scattered about her. A tiny scrap lay in a crease in her lap and her heart beat faster. She pressed her finger to it and turned it over. His face looked up from the paper. "He loves me. . ." she whispered. She knew it inside, hugged it to her clamshell — tight, so it had to be true.

A beady-eyed seagull landed on the open window and squawked. She could see right down its throat, past its mean yellow beak with a red splotch like a bloodstain. "Get away!" Sass clapped her hands and jumped up, and the bird took off with a noisy cry.

Why did Alex care so much about what people thought? Wasn't he used to it? The reporters at the gate were scary, but they were kind of doing a job. People didn't think about gossip for long, did they? They just repeated it, or didn't think much about it at all. It wasn't like she was anyone special. Was she?

Not like he was.

Alex had said that secrets were the best and worst. What did that mean? Because if their secret was out, then the worst had happened. Couldn't they just get back to being the best? Or was he just using this as an excuse to break up?

She kicked off her bedding and swung her feet out of bed; tugged on her jeans and a sweater. He was a prince. That complicated matters, but really, get over it! Nobody had died.

Sass threw a pillow off the bed, which bumped an easel that took out a canvas, and they all went crashing to the floor. There was only one way to find out how he felt about her. If she went to the meadow, then Alex might come, and then ... she'd know. It was time to take a deep breath and face him.

She opened the boat-shed loft door a crack, cautious of reporters. A bunch of them were sitting on the harbour wall like gulls hoping to be fed. She closed it again and climbed out the back window. Outside, the sky was a purple bruise as Sass ran over the hill and to the gates of Trist. Without the key, the wall needed climbing, and the ivy was slippery from yesterday's rain. Cobwebs glistened and the thorns of a bramble rose clutched at her clothes as she made it to the other side where the meadow was the same kind of beautiful, only wetter and emptier without Bo. And yet, some magical thread still wound her in. She couldn't stay away. Alex would come, wouldn't he? They'd kiss and make up. And all would be right with the world.

It was late afternoon when Amy swept the yard; Figgy had been at her all day. Do this, do that, had she done the hay nets, scrubbed the feed bowls, poo-picked the paddocks, checked on the foals? The list was endless. Muck shoveller, that was her. No wonder Alex had stopped noticing.

He'd gone back to London, his tail between his legs. She reached for the note in her pocket, the one that he'd asked her to give to that girl, Saskia. Not Plum but the "mystery mermaid" all over the Internet. Amy squirmed; she hadn't peeked, and it was almost killing her. She knew it wasn't hers, but if she handed it over now after waiting, like, hours, how would that look? Maybe she could say she hadn't been able to get away, which was sort of true. Amy glanced down at the smudged boy scrawl. Say that she couldn't make out the address: Sass c/o Chapel Gallery. Clear as day. It wasn't fair. Nobody had seen or heard of the girl before now. In the paper, her face was hidden, but Amy had seen it when Saskia Emerson got back from that ride on Bo yesterday. Amy's heart hardened. Poor horse was tired out. The girl's hair had been dripping wet, and her T-shirt had gone see-through. Bad as that dress hanging open. She was famous now, or the back of her head was. She didn't think that Alex had it in him to cheat on Plum — not the lying type. Or even in some small way on her: Amy Smith, the girl who, once upon a time, he'd wanted. She knew because she'd seen it in his face enough times.

Alex had stood in front of her this morning with the note in his hand when she — Amy — was the one who knew how much he hated it in London, how his face changed every time he got on Dancer after being stuck at school. She understood because she hated school too. Not that hers was posh like his. Hers was a dump and she wasn't going back.

Saskia Emerson. Not even pretty. Yeah, okay, nice legs, big eyes, but if Alex wanted ordinary, he could have had *her*. Samey Amy who'd always be there for him, and loved Dancer and Bo like they were her own. She scrunched the note in her pocket. She wouldn't pass it on. Not yet. It wasn't the end of the world. Was it?

One good thing. Plum was stewed. Sweet as custard and just as dumb.

32

NACHOS UNHAPPINESS

Sass shook out the rug that she'd brought from the boat-shed loft and sat at the edge, waiting, fidgeting, wishing that Alex would come. She shifted position; she'd been there forever already and her legs were pins and needles. Her stomach rumbled. She'd brought a bag of crisps to share, like this was some picnic, but it had split, and blown four ways to the wind. Nachos unhappiness. A chilly dampness was soaking through the seat of her pants.

Where was he? She'd so believed that he'd come.

She waited for maybe another hour, then stood up. Her legs felt oddly weak. He wasn't coming, not today. He'd get word to her if he wanted. She walked down to the creek and threw a pebble in the water which glinted darkly in the fading afternoon light.

"Come on, Alex," she murmured, slipping a little in the mud: even a message in a bottle would be nice.

Sass began to walk back, shivering in the drizzle as she trailed the wet throw behind her. What had she expected? That he'd be waiting for her with his arms out? She'd felt so sure it was just a huge misunderstanding, that he'd realise and come. But then Alex wasn't like other boys. And it was *his* face that was everywhere. Words written about her were soon forgotten; a photo of him was worth a thousand of those.

Sass returned to an empty cottage. David and Jessie had an opening at the gallery. On the fridge in the kitchen was a note with her name on. She didn't know who squeaked louder, her or Harry, when she stepped on him in her rush to reach it. Please let it be from Alex.

Fish pie inside. Thirty minutes, 200 C. Don't be too hard on yourself. Back soon. Big hug. J & D x

Sass stuffed the dish in the oven and sat down. A thumbed copy of the *Daily Sun* lay across the table. She reached over and picked it up.

PRINCESS OF SMILES STEPS OUT

Sources close to the palace have revealed that the divorce of their Royal Highnesses will be announced tomorrow. Silencing her critics, the Princess stepped out at a gala for one of her favourite charities, Prison Relief. The Princess looked "stunning" in a demure, floor-length crêpe de Chine dress by Chloe Taylor-Warnes, an up-and-coming British designer. A spokesperson confirmed that the tiny seed pearls around her collar and cuffs were hand-embroidered by a

sewing group of talented inmates at Wormwood Scrubs.
Cressida Slater reporting.

So at least she was old news, Sass thought. That was good, though it still went on for Alex, his life spread out every day. Sass put a hand to her chest, feeling the familiar tug at her heart; at least her mom was safe in here. Sass would never have fitted in his world anyway. Stupid to expect him to even show up. She was the girl you took for dim sum on the Lower East Side, not to a palace banquet.

Sass glanced back at the paper. Just how many photos of the royal family were out there? If you stuck them all on a wall, would you fill a palace? Her thoughts strayed up the stairs to the old snapshot she'd seen in David and Jessie's bedroom. The one of the young soldier who'd looked so like her. Who was he? Suddenly Sass wanted to know, even if it was another dead face to put to the family name.

In the upstairs bedroom, the sprig of lilac had gone, replaced by a rose in a teacup. Full-blown, it was losing its bloom, but its fragrance still filled the untidy space. Sass put on a bedside lamp and there, leaning against a pile of paperbacks, dusted in a powder of light, was the photo in its frame.

Sass picked it up and peered at it more closely. Looking at it again, she could see quite clearly that it wasn't a group of young soldiers at all but an aircrew. Who else would wear lifejackets over thick leather coats? And that shadowy thing behind them had to be the metal wing of a plane? She squinted at the face of the young man again. He still looked like her, or was it the other way around? At least she hadn't imagined it. Was his name on the back? She'd open it to see.

The catches on the leather frame were tightly closed and lightly rusted. Sass took out a nail file and prised them open. It took some force, but the frame sprang apart undamaged, and a flattened roll of silver ribbon tumbled out. How odd and beautiful, and a little sad? She held up the frayed end of the silver coil and let it unfurl, watching it twist and spin in the air.

Returning to the photo, Sass saw that it had slipped out and floated under the bed. She got on her hands and knees to retrieve it from a heap of dust balls. In faded blue ink on the back, someone had written a name, a place and a date: Jack, Cornwall '43.

"I see you've met Grandpa?"

David stood in the doorway. Sass hadn't heard him come in.

She looked up, full of questions that only he, the last man standing in her family, could possibly answer.

"I had a — grandpa, here in Cornwall?"

"A great-grandpa. Not so unlikely, when you think about it."

"I don't understand; he was American?"

"He was, but it was during the war. Jack Rigby was stationed here, along with thousands of others, mostly infantry. GIs. He was different: an officer pilot, bomber aircrew. He's one of the reasons that I came here. I wanted to find out about him, or to see where he died."

David chewed his lip as if there were more he could have added.

"My great-grandpa died, over here?"

"Uh-huh. I'm afraid so. His plane crashed in the sea, somewhere over the Channel. The crew never made it back from Germany." David shrugged. "Most didn't."

Sass swallowed, her eyes swimming with unexpected tears that she tried to blink back.

"His name's different from ours."

"That's easy. His daughter. My mother. Your grandmother. Changed her name when she married."

"And do you think this was hers too?" Sass held up the ribbon, which quivered in her fingers. David took it from her, smoothing the band of silk with his thumb. It was obvious he hadn't seen it before.

"Where did you find this?"

"It was hidden in the back of the photo frame."

"I never knew. I guess it must have meant something to him. Some kind of memento. He was very young, no more than nineteen, and newly married with my mother on the way. Shotgun wedding to my grandmother, apparently." David smiled softly. "They threw caution to the wind when war was declared. From what I heard, it was a brief and unhappy marriage. They weren't at all suited. And then of course he died. The photo must have come back with his things."

A wave of emotion tipped Sass off balance. She rocked on her feet and David caught her shoulders.

Too much, too much. She didn't want to hear any more. Couldn't something she touched go right?

33

AN INVITATION

The days rolled by. No note from Alex. No message in a bottle. No signal fire from a cliff top. No sound of midnight hooves or sign of a lantern light in a tower. No sail, black or white. Just a steady drizzle that marked each passing hour. Even the cluster of hard-core photographers had gone now, prised from their rocks. In that respect, the weather had been kind.

Sass was still in her dressing-gown when the sound of a car interrupted her thoughts. She threw down her book and flew to the window.

Had he come at last?

Instead the old guy in the peaked hat, who'd driven her home from the church, left the motor running and walked up to the cottage.

Maybe Alex had found out where she lived?

She wanted to lean out and shout, "Hey, hello, I'm up here?" but "chauffeur guy" had already knocked at the front door of the cottage, and by the time she'd thrown on some clothes and burst into the kitchen, he'd gone, and Jessie and David were talking over their morning coffee.

"What took you so long?" said David with a half smile, pushing something across the table.

Shaky-fingered, Sass picked up a small white card.

Please, please, she murmured in her head. Please be from him.

No bigger than a bus ticket, the card could fit in the palm of her hand. Holding her breath, she glanced down.

Lady Helena Tremayne

At Home

It wasn't from Alex. Sass sat down, her chair scraping on the tiles. She turned it over and read the spidery, slightly unsteady handwriting on the back:

Dear Saskia,
   Would love you to ride Bo. Come for tea on Friday. Four o'clock sharp.
   Corbett will collect you.
   Helena

Sass whispered the mare's name. Bo would make her feel better. Bo made everything better. She took a deep breath and exhaled with a sigh: Bo, her gentle, silver horse.

And Alex? Alex was bound to be there at the house and they'd say sorry to each other in a very English way, and then...

"Will you go?" Jessie interrupted.

Sass picked at her sleeve. "Sure, why shouldn't I?"

"Sass, you know why not. There's been no word from him for days. Prince or not, he's only up the road. Hasn't he..."

Sass felt a prickle, which she pushed stubbornly back.

"*She's* invited me. It's my decision if I go, isn't it?"

Jessie got up and put her mug in the sink.

"Of course." She paused, leaning on her hands. "Just be careful, love. We don't want you to get any more hurt."

Cressida Slater sharpened her nails. Until now she'd had a French manicure with the tips squared off, but this press conference was too unbelievably tedious. Honestly, just when she'd revealed who Mermaid Girl was, she was summoned back to London. For what? The DIV — she yawned — ORCE. Waiting at BP for announcements was such a bore: Buckingham Palace, to the plebs outside. Even the queen had chosen to stay at Balmoral. Who could blame her? This time, though, the royal flunkies were deliberately keeping them waiting. Bad idea when stories with deadlines had a habit of writing themselves.

Cressida looked around at the assembled camera crews from across the globe, waved her nail file at a handsome broadcaster from *America Tonight*, whose name she'd forgotten. A divorce didn't sell like a royal baby, or the dream ticket, a royal wedding. Unless the family put in an appearance? The princess knew the value of good press, even if her soon-to-be ex was – Cressida yawned again – so utterly last century.

While she was in London, she'd get an intern on to researching ... what was her name? Cressida smirked. She knew it by heart, but loved seeing it in print.

Saskia Laura Emerson. Not a local girl at all. She'd found that much out. As for young Prince Charming, #palacealex was trending wildly and she'd only just begun. She'd dig up more on this girl if it was the last thing she did. Cressida had a nose for romance and a heart as hard as stone.

In the end, there was no photocall for Alex. His mother had wanted one, but his father had backed out; flatly refused and said he "wasn't having his son mauled again by the media." So, that was it. Just a depressing announcement by a red-faced prime minister. Alex wondered darkly if the woman didn't have better things to do, like run a country?

The rain dripped down the apartment window, blurring the lights of London. Had his leaving saved Sass from anything? He'd kept his head down and nothing more had been reported, though the pictures were still everywhere. The palace lawyers had swung into action. It was a busy summer for them.

Alex had spent more time with his father in the last few days than ever before in his life. They were like castaways waiting to be rescued. They'd be eating each other soon. More alike than either of them realised. Private. Stubborn. Stranded. Mum had swum for it. He didn't blame her. She'd kissed him and said she loved him, but was going away until it all died down. Eduardo had offered her the "sanctuary" of his Argentine ranch, something about the lushness of his "pampas". Alex didn't ask.

In Cornwall, they called rain "mizzle", as in mist and drizzle. He could see Sass in Bo's stable, water trickling down her neck. If he closed his eyes, he could feel the dampness of her T-shirt and the warmth of her heart. He banged his head once against the glass, then twice.

He missed her.

34

TEA WITH A COUNTESS

What should she wear to see the boy she liked, take tea with a countess and go riding? It wasn't the sort of thing they taught you in magazines. Sass felt hot and anxious just thinking about it. She hung her things on David's easel, switching tops with her jeans. The kimono jacket was too ... unusual; Mom's sweater ... not right. The plaid shirt too ... plaid. She settled for a borrowed blue cami of Jessie's.

The car arrived for her at 3.45 p.m. "B" for Bentley with a pair of fancy silver wings. Sass felt queasy just creaking across the leather. She rolled down the window to get some air and give Jessie and David an easy wave that she really wasn't feeling. Her hands shook and a small twitch flickered at the side of her eye. Not good: winking at a countess.

Fifteen minutes later and still holding her breath, Sass looked up through the windscreen at Trist. Dorothy at the gates of the Emerald City. After the movie, Mom had read her the book from cover to cover. Her fingerprints would still be there. A brush and a little detective dust, and she'd see them turning the pages.

The car drew up and Sass reached for the door handle, but Corbett shook his head in the mirror and came around the side to open it. He really didn't have to.

"Just pull the bell rope and go in. Her Ladyship is in the kitchen. She's expecting you."

"Oh, okay. Thank you for the ride."

Sass walked in. She'd never been inside, only come close, of course.

The house was like a great overcoat: scuffed and battered, the colour of wax, and lined with the warmest wool.

A threadbare Persian rug of faded pink led her over the flagstones in the hallway, past an umbrella stand of extraordinary walking sticks, to an oak dresser weighed down with beautiful things: keys, a peacock feather, flowers and a bust in an old straw hat. Sass tiptoed to the foot of a wood-panelled staircase, where a grandfather clock stood sentry, ticking in time with her heart.

Where was Alex? Hadn't he heard her arrive? She'd felt sure that he'd be waiting. In her head she could see him standing there, self-conscious in breeches and socks and a shirt with a collar. She tried to imagine the expression on his face. Happy or aloof? Awkward or pleased? Would he reach out and hug her? Tug her into some corner, or keep her at arm's length? What would they say to each other; would "sorry" begin to cover it? Sass loitered in the hall for as long as she dared before following the smell of baking toward the kitchen. She couldn't eat a thing.

The Countess was sitting at a vast scrubbed table in the biggest kitchen in the world. She was cleaning boots: short ones and long, dressed in a stained artist's smock over a flamingo-pink blouse with a pie-frill neck. Sass wondered if she should curtsy or something to make up for last time? She tried a weak smile instead.

"My dear, you're here. Don't hover in the doorway; do come in."

A pile of clothing sat at the end of a painted bench: pale gloves, pale cotton shirt, pale breeches, a pair of newly shined black boots, and on the top ... What was that? Sass stepped back a little. A spider. No. She peered closer. Was that ... a hairnet?

"If you're going to ride, you must be dressed properly. These days, our fellow Europeans rather outshine us, even if they are a little lavish with the diamanté." Helena shuddered slightly. Sass wasn't sure if she meant the bling, or the thought of being European instead of British.

Sass's gaze shifted beyond her. Come on, Alex, I need you here. His things were everywhere and yet *he* wasn't. Sass couldn't think straight, let alone make polite conversation. She sat down and twisted her hands in an abandoned sweater that might have been his.

"I — Is Alex coming?" Her words fell straight over the kcrb of good manners.

The countess looked down her nose as if she'd half expected the question.

"My dear, Alex isn't here." She leaned forward and patted Sass's hand, her palm as dry as paper. "He had to go off to London. All terribly sudden. I expect you've seen the ncws about the divorce? A sad business."

"Yes — No — I — It's just —" Sass squeezed her hands into fists to stop them from betraying her.

"Knowing my errant grandson —" the old lady gave a tight smile — "he would have wanted you to carry on riding Bo, even without him. He told me as much himself."

"He did?" Sass's heart surged, then contracted, as the meaning of her words sank in. "Will he be gone long, in London?" Her voice a whisper, as if he'd gone to the ends of the earth. She knew what was being said; she wasn't stupid. Alex had gone for good and it stung with a pain that took her breath away. Helena had invited her here out of sympathy, that much was clear. Maybe he knew when he was better off without her. She was an embarrassment, after all. Maybe instead he'd gone back to Plum?

"My dear." There was a long pause as Helena read her mind. "Sometimes one must make do without. Now I think it's time you got changed." She patted the pile of riding clothes. "We'll take tea on the lawn afterwards."

Helena leaned against the side of the arena where the horses were schooled. She was used to her own company, but had missed her grandson almost immediately. She'd watched Alexander change in just a few weeks from a surly boy into a tanned and rather dashing young man. Heaven-sent, he was a prince of the realm. Helena smiled, awfully biased. He simply had no idea. She'd seen Amy looking, of course. Had Alex noticed the darting glances? Boys were so blind on occasion, and now her grandson had fallen for this girl, Saskia.

Her thoughts turned to the teenager blinking back the news of Alex's departure. Helena hadn't mentioned how he'd dashed off in the mistaken belief that if all eyes were on him and his wretched parents, the press might leave her alone. Because would they? Helena rather doubted it. There hadn't been time for proper goodbyes; Alex's face so shut down. Still, she thought firmly, it was probably better that any relationship ended now, rather than with more tears later.

Her opinion on her grandson's upbringing had never been sought by the palace. An irony given that Trist was his chosen home. After more than seventy years, Helena was still in exile. Cast off at eighteen for her own scandalous behaviour, which to her at the time had simply, and overwhelmingly, felt like love.

What did she think? That Alex was better off in London at some ghastly "photocall"? Piggy in the middle of a horrid divorce. She understood, of course, that without a show of civilised togetherness, they were all of them lost, especially in this age. It was a lesson that Alex had to learn: that however much you hurt inside, you put on a brave public face. It was his duty. His noble destiny. So marvellously, miserably British.

And yet, what was to be done with this young American left behind? Twice now, Helena had seen the confusion on her face. Didn't she have a duty to protect her? Keep an eye on her and make sure that at the very least, she learned to ride? If she could handle a horse, then she could handle almost anything. Helena sighed. Nothing beat a good western. Those rugged men riding off into the sunset. Such wonderful hats.

She watched as Figgy led Bo in: twenty metres of canvas lunge line attached to the mare's bit. The horse stood like a saint as Saskia stepped forward and stroked Bo's brow. Figgy's response was predictably brusque as she wound up her knitting. Figgy came from a long line of colonials who'd put entire nations to the test.

"Stand to the left of her, gather up your reins, put your foot in the stirrup and hop on."

Undaunted, the girl sprang up with a lightness that was surprising. She sat there waiting, as if she'd ridden all her life. Figgy ventured the question rather loudly.

"Done much of this, have you?"

Helena grimaced. Figgy had a heart of gold, but a certain way with words.

"No, only a few times..." Saskia's eyes cast down. "Once with Alex. You saw us, remember?"

"Ah, yes. How could I forget. You're sitting well now. Nice and straight."

"Bo makes it easy." The girl bent forward and smoothed the mare's neck from the tips of her ears down to the crest of her mane. Figgy seemed to visibly soften. A chink in her armour: anyone who appreciated Bo.

"Okay now, sit tight and hold on to the front of the saddle. I have control from here in the centre as she moves round in a circle. Let Bo do all the work."

And she did: walk, trot and canter. They flowed together well, quite effortlessly, as if the girl was swimming on horseback. She'd even closed her eyes and held out her arms, almost balance-perfect.

Helena raised her hand from the side, her bones creaking as she pushed herself from the fence and walked over.

"Thank you, Figgy. I'll take it from here."

In a paddock in the shade of the house, Bo nudged at Sass's pockets. Sass had loved, *loved* her lesson with the Countess. She wanted to learn and Helena knew so much. Riding was something that maybe she could do. She couldn't go back to swimming. Not without Mom. But riding felt right. If only Alex had been there to see her. Sass rubbed her face and found that her eyes, and nose, were running: the dust and hay must have got to her.

"Silly!" she murmured. Who was she kidding? Only herself.

She slipped off Bo's halter and sat on the grass, and let herself think about Mom and Alex and the great-grandfather she never knew. And allowed herself to cry, for just a little while.

As she dried her eyes, she watched the horse who had brought her here amble across the paddock to a water trough. Bo drank deeply, ears flicking, her tail whisking at flies, and in the quiet beyond hearing, Sass found peace.

Tomorrow and the week after that, Helena had invited her back, and she'd do it again. And though Mom and Alex weren't here, she had Bo, and Jessie and David, and Harry, and Helena, and even Figgy. She could get past this, couldn't she?

35

LONG DAYS

For the next week and a half, Sass moved on. No longer hanging on to the saddle to balance, she was off the long lunge line and telling Bo where to go with subtle shifts of her hands, legs and weight. Walk, trot, canter, each of them separate and then put together.

"For goodness' sake," Helena would exclaim, "be clear with Bo. Don't pull her in the mouth. Carry your reins, sit up and half halt . . . Yes, that's better, but make sure you're sitting deep. Shoulders back. Super."

Diagonals, circles, loops and serpentines came next: movements that meant something to her now. A whole new language of equitation. And although it wasn't really dressage, Bo responded sweetly, even when Sass messed up, which was often.

Helena kept her so busy, Sass could almost pretend that she'd moved on from Alex. And when she wasn't riding, she helped with Bo. Figgy showed her how to pick the mare's feet out with a hoof pick. How to wash Bo off when she was sweaty, how to put a stable sheet over her so that she'd dry sooner, and just how much hay was enough.

And the days went by. The only person who was never really friendly was the other stable girl, Amy, who rode out by herself on Dancer. Once or twice, Sass caught her eye and smiled, but the girl would scuttle away, brush the yard harder or fork the muck heap higher.

Maybe she had her own stuff to deal with? Sass got that. After Mom died, people would turn away from her, uncomfortable. Was that how Alex thought about her now? His face was getting less clear in her head, although every day she stumbled across his things. Little things. And then her heart would beat faster. A pair of his riding gloves. A paper bag of tangerines on a chair in the tack room. Rosettes on the wall that Figgy would list as his: in red, blue, green and yellow. And when Sass drank her tea, his dog, Susan would rest her nose in her lap because she missed him too.

In the Kensington apartment, Alex mooched from room to room. It was cluttered with packing boxes and crates because his mother had moved out and her stuff was soon to follow. The staff still had loads more to do; there were wardrobes full of her clothes. And hats. Endless bloody hats. He spun one across the drawing room like a Frisbee on the beach.

Now school had officially ended, everyone had gone home or abroad or both. He saw the stream of updates on Facebook, including pictures of Gully and Ol messing about in Ibiza. By the end of the week, he'd caught up entirely on Netflix, was bored of his Xbox, and was left with his music and earphones.

Going quietly mad.

The talk of his parents was keeping the media busy. Alex checked his phone for the millionth time. Kept going back to that one picture of Sass; now he had Wi-Fi and a signal, it was almost impossible not to.

Nothing more had been reported since he left, so maybe his taking the heat had worked. Even so, every time he remembered her face, he wished things could've been different. He glanced at the emblazoned box of white stationery on his father's desk. Should he write her a proper letter? She'd have received his scribble by now. His phone pinged: Google Alerts. Alex's eyes flicked down the screen.

And what he saw there made him want to throw up.

36

ALL AT SEA

Cressida sank her teeth into the warm heaped scone, jam and clotted cream oozing from the corners of her mouth. With a flick of her tongue, she caught a fallen strawberry and eyed the last scoop of cream in the pot. Go on, you're worth it! She sucked the silver teaspoon clean.

She was staying somewhere decent in Cornwall this time, though the weather was dismal. She glanced across the bay, where a flotilla of blue-and-white boats from a local yacht club was racing toward a flag, first around the buoy. How very apt. The outcry to her latest reveal was spectacular, sales had gone crazy. Everyone was talking, except for the tight-lipped palace press office, when it was their own fault really. They should've been more helpful.

Once she'd seen Saskia's name and face in that sketch, the rest of her research had been easy, helped not least by the knuckleheaded landlord in the pub, who'd let slip not just about the uncle's name and the Chapel Gallery connection, but that he was originally a New Yorker to boot. So she'd started in the Big Apple with a private investigator she knew, an ex-cop called Al Bull, and what he'd dug up was the ultimate scoop. A tear-jerker. A story sadder than Bambi. Even for an old hack like her, the police report was disturbing. Cressida quivered. What she'd done wasn't strictly "ethical", but her journalist's pointy nail was always going to press "SEND". It was her job: mistakes and misery, her speciality.

LITTLE MERMAID ALL AT SEA. PRINCE'S TRAGIC HOLIDAY GIRL

Cressida Slater reporting.

Helena sat in the drawing room with her morning elevenses, listening to the trees bend and sigh outside. A storm was rising, the bones of the house had begun to rattle, and yesterday, high fish-scale clouds had told of the old mariner's warning: A mackerel in the sky, not three days dry.

Time to batten down the hatches. She closed the photograph album that she'd pulled out to show Saskia later. Nobody made albums like these any more. This one had a hand-marbled cover and thick cream pages, and a spine of crimson leather. Such a fiddle mounting photos the old way, but when she turned the pages, Helena was there again with Bo just after she was born: her wobbly, knobbly-kneed filly, who she'd named in memory of the boy Helena had loved, and lost, almost three quarters of a century ago.

There was a knock at the door. A top-up at last? Helena held out the empty teapot, but instead Corbett handed her a tray with that ghastly rag rolled up on it: the Daily Sun. What nonsensical wickedness was it spouting today?

"Take it away, Corbett. You know better than to bring me *that*."

He coughed and shifted uneasily.

"If I may be permitted, Your Ladyship, you may wish to see this?"

"Why ever. . .?"

She took it from him and shook it open. Her words a splutter of outrage.

"How awful. How utterly dreadful! How dare they? How low will that woman stoop?"

Poor Corbett backed away.

Alex leaned forward, straining against his seat belt, both hands on the dashboard. He could barely see through the thick sea mist. Two weeks he'd been away. Two weeks that felt like a year.

When Jim had confirmed the news of Sass to him in the early hours of this morning, Alex had come. His bodyguard was next to him at the wheel. Not so much a friend as a solid shadow. He was staying on at Trist, but right now there was only one person Alex wanted to be with, because what the Daily Sun was reporting blew his mind.

Sass.

He'd had no idea.

With a slow and awful clearness, Alex remembered his grandmother's careful words: "Saskia doesn't need any more heartache."

When they split, he'd been angry, stupid and arrogant, but now he saw that his ego hardly mattered. There was another explanation for the shadows beneath Sass's lashes. Why he'd found her in a meadow with a horse as kind as Bo; the reason she couldn't seem to breathe when she'd told him about herself. Galloping before she could ride. Something had happened in her life earlier. Something bad that she couldn't talk about. And now the whole world knew because of Who. He. Was.

"Jim, I'm getting out, I need some air." His hand was on the car-door handle. *Happier than ever before*, the first newspaper story had said about her, and he'd thrown it back in Sass's face. He had to find her; to tell her that he loved her. That he'd stand by her through all this!

"You'll have to catch me first!" She had shouted in the sea. And he had — then dropped her like a stone.

"Sit still, Alex," Jim said levelly, his foot to the accelerator. "You're not going anywhere, not yet. We're expected at Trist and the weather's closing in."

Alex shut his eyes and saw Sass peering through the

hedge into his world. Standing in the trailer like a gawky deer. The tear streaks that he'd missed, or maybe he'd have noticed if he hadn't been so into himself. And now this. Cressida Slater's latest "reveal", a leaked accident investigation report. So real it made him feel physically sick. Black-and-white photographs of the upside-down carcass of a delivery van. Zigzag-parked emergency vehicles. A police cordon and two big arrows with accompanying distances pointing to a chalk outline where a forty-seven-year-old mother was killed on a busy New York pavement, shielding her teenage daughter.

Sass didn't know "the full story" until later that morning. Until then, she'd been okay: really, she had. Jessie and David had done their best to keep it from her, but at lunchtime she'd overheard them talking, so she'd stolen Jessie's phone from her purse and found out for herself. She'd climbed a hill until a signal reached her like a laser beam and then so much had leaked out of that tiny screen. A haemorrhage of hurt, and pain and guilt. Why would anyone want to know her sad story? Because she'd kissed a prince?

In themselves, the photos were nothing: just grimly clinical police shots. The kind kept on some official file. Not like in a big TV drama where everyone in the courtroom covered their mouths in shock-horror. This was what a real crash scene looked like after the dead people had gone. Lumps of twisted metal, strange arrows and skid marks. Just another forensic day for real-life investigators.

By then she'd been in the hospital. And Mom. Where had they taken Mom? She'd tried to find out and it was a while before she knew.

Sass sat on the wet grass and let the rain drip down her face. Why was all this happening? Had she been too happy too soon? Or was the truth much simpler? That she deserved all this because ... because she should have died instead.

37

WRECKERS

Sass thought of going to the meadow to hide. A trickle of light had seeped into her mind: a mental picture of sunshine, a grey pony's nose, a wild cluster of strawberries and a musty horse trailer with an imprint of a boy on a campbed, where she could curl up for a hundred years. Her head was aching and her heart was drained; she was too young for all this.

Head down in the wind, Sass missed the muddy turn inland, and pretty soon she was past the beach too: the place where she'd galloped and been kissed. Both mistakes, she saw now.

David had told her about Cornish smugglers long ago and it had sounded so romantic; all kegs of French brandy and bolts of silk and lace she'd read. But she'd seen about wreckers too. People who lured ships onto rocks with flaming lanterns. She imagined the cries of sailors, the sound of tearing canvas and the crack of a falling mast.

The world divided into wreckers, survivors and the drowned. But which one was she?

Sass turned away from the broken image and shaded her face from the wind-whipped spray, her ears filled with the sound of the sea. Her eyes travelled up to the top of the ridge that loomed above the path she was standing on, where a dark silhouette seemed to defy gravity as if in some deal with the weather. The tower. She'd stood there with Alex and looked dizzily down. If she could find a way up, that was where she would go.

It was a steep climb. Sass hung on to the roots of squat trees and bushes, and as the black stack came nearer, she remembered her first excitement at seeing the turret with Alex. History not so much peeping through paint cracks as leaning out and waving for all to see. Now the tower seemed to float in a moat of wet mist. Pushing on the last few feet, Sass staggered inside the doorway, where she sat with her back to the wall and her knees drawn up, the noise in her head switched off at last.

No more wind and sea, or shouts and sirens. This was the place where Alex had touched her and whispered about stories of hopeless love, his hands at her back. Was she ready to climb the stairs on her own to see for herself?

Sass stepped into the stairwell. Hugging the central pillar, she crept up the crooked steps. And when she was so far from the bottom that she could scarcely look down, she scrambled the rest of the way on her hands and knees, her focus on the circle of light ahead.

As she emerged from the darkness, a great gust of wind caught her and she cowered away from the edge, keeping her back and her heels to the wall, until she reached the place where Alex had lifted her onto her toes and whispered about Tristan and Iseult.

Her hands flat to the cold stone behind her, she inched around until she was directly opposite a crumbled, tooth-like gap that yawned over the drop below. It had been blustery the last time she stood there, but now the wind was screaming through it.

There had been no happy ending for Tristan and Iseult, so why did she think that she and Alex could work out? Why had Alex even told her about them? It was as if he *knew*. Sass bit her lip and felt herself burn up. She stood up and faced her fear, and inside felt angry.

How dare he think she'd have given their secret away! How dare he not listen and leave her like this!

She pulled at the neck of his stupid sweatshirt, the one she still wore. One sleeve at a time, she wrestled it off, frightening herself when, hood-like, it still covered her head, and she imagined the brush of a gull sending her tumbling forward.

Think, Sass, think.

A black sail for her. Alex wasn't coming back. She balled up the top and threw it. A feel-good moment that soon passed. Her only question now ... the real question: should she stay, or fly to some other place? She looked down into the gaping space.

The call came on the landline at about two o'clock in the afternoon. Corbett answered it and Alex knew it was serious the moment the butler came over and whispered in his grandmother's ear.

"What is it, Grandma?" Alex stopped pacing.

"It's Saskia," she murmured. "It seems she's — run away."

Alex was out of there. Gone. The great front door slamming behind him.

He dragged on his old drover's coat and boots in the tackroom. He looked for the keys to the quad bike, but they'd gone from their usual place. Dancer's bridle was hanging on a nearby hook. He couldn't ride him, not this time, but he could take Bo. Steady, reliable Bo.

The mare was surprised to be treated so roughly; it wasn't what she was used to. She flattened her ears when the unfamiliar bit went in her mouth and Alex led her out of the stable. No time to saddle up, he vaulted onto her back and kicked her straight into a gallop. She answered, thundering down the grassy park in a thud of mud and flying turf, her hooves forging with sparks. His hands stayed light on the wet reins, which were slippery to hold, and the veins in her neck bulged with the effort. Alex had some idea of where Sass might have gone, the places he'd have chosen. Three possibilities: the meadow, the beach or the tower. Anywhere else, he didn't want to think about.

Bo slid down the path from the top of the meadow, she was blowing hard. It wasn't late in the afternoon, but the daylight had fused in the wet. Alex jumped off by the trailer, shocked to see how high the creek had risen. Taking the reins over Bo's head, he went to the door. Was Sass in there? His eyes took a while to adjust, but when they did, he could see that it was empty.

Biting back his disappointment, he remounted. He stroked Bo's neck and withers. The old horse was tired, but he still urged her down the long track by the creek to the beach. Water slopped over the top of the banks and the going was soft and boggy.

In contrast, the beach was a cold blast of emptiness — almost impossible to sit upright. Tufts of grass lay flattened on the sand dunes and everywhere was a swirling mass of grit. The light was beginning to run out and the only place left was the tower. Alex's throat went tight.

Why would she go up there? She'd been frightened enough the first time. "I'm not a fan of heights!" she'd half laughed, but he'd made her go up the turret, desperate to impress without even knowing it.

Bo shied away when Alex turned her onto a coast path that was never meant for horses. She reeled back until he made her go there, his hands gripping her mane, his heels hard at her sides as her hooves slipped on the rockiest parts, the sea waiting below them.

At a copse of bent trees, Alex turned off the narrow track and followed a sheep's path up onto the ridge. Bo scrambled up, grateful to have grass beneath her feet, and through the thorny gorse, Alex could see the tower ahead.

Be there, he willed. He was all out of chances.

At the summit, he left Bo in the shelter of the wall. Stepping inside the low stone archway, he called out Sass's name.

"Sass? Sass are you in here?" he shouted, afraid when only his voice echoed back. As his eyes adapted, he saw a huddle at the foot of the stairs. Oh god, had she fallen?

"Sass? Is that you?"

"Alex?" The huddle moved.

"Yes, it's me," he said, as he ran over and took her hand. "You're here . . . you came to find me?"

He stroked her hair. "Did you think I wouldn't?"

"Not after what I did — what you said —" She sat up and he could see the whites of her eyes in the darkness.

"I should never have left, but I've come for you now, if you'll let me."

Turning to him, she took a deep breath. "I didn't tell you about —"

"I know what happened to your mother."

"You read it?"

"Yes." He felt ashamed. The accident report in the paper. He shouldn't have looked.

"I wanted you to hear it from me, but I didn't know how to say it."

Her face was so open, the fear written on her forehead.

She reached out for his hand, her fingers even colder than his. "I'm here, not just for the summer, but maybe forever. In England, at least. My mom died. It's true. She was in a car wreck a few months back. We were arguing over nothing — hair conditioner. Imagine? The chlorine, you see, from swim training —"

Her voice trailed off.

"I was sulking in the street, so I didn't have to walk next to her on the sidewalk —" she hung her head "— like a stupid baby, when this truck, this big truck came around the corner too fast. And Mom — Mom —" Sass doubled over and buried her face in her lap. "She pulled me out of the way but then this car — skidded to avoid the truck, and it —" Her voice tightly muffled. "She died, so I could live. It was my fault, don't you see?"

Alex wrapped his arms around her and she hugged him back, squeezing the breath from his chest. "No, Sass. It wasn't your fault. It was just a terrible accident."

"I pretended that I was okay, but I wasn't, and then when you went I missed you so much —"

"Sass, I should never have left. I'm so very sorry."

"You — you're always apologising." A watery smile.

Something like love made him braver. He took her hands; he wanted to warm them. He kissed the base of her thumb and leaned forward. They bumped noses. They touched lips. His on hers, breathing her in.

"You're freezing," he said, as she curled in his arms like a cockle in a shell.

Outside the wind fought with the trees that seemed to twist around the tower and keep it upright. Bo stamped her foot, tired of waiting.

Alex looked up when he heard the shrill whinny. "Sass, it's time to go."

"You brought Dancer with you?"

"No, it's Bo."

That seemed to lift her.

He took off his coat and put it on her, caught Bo's reins and hoisted Sass onto the horse's back. He'd take her home the quickest way he knew, the most direct route, the steep track that wound back down and along the creek to Trist.

38

THE FLOOD

Down they went, following the brown smear that had once been a bridle path. Halfway down, Sass slid off Bo; it was impossible to ride her with the mud sucking at her feet. Besides, it wasn't fair; she and Alex could lead her home.

But when they reached the edge of the creek, neither of them could believe their eyes. The fat twisted thing that met them was no longer the stream of daydreams. Gorged with water, the creek reminded her of a boa constrictor that she'd once seen at a zoo. It had slithered down behind its glass wall to be fed dead mice by its keeper, its belly stretched and bloated.

Not far from the horse trailer, Bo planted her feet and refused to go any farther. She lifted her head in the air with her nostrils flared and snorted at whatever was spooking her.

Alex tugged wearily at the reins.

"Come on, Bo, it's nothing, get on with it!"

Wiping at her face, Sass thought she heard a sound too.

"What's that? Can you hear it?"

"I don't know. Thunder, maybe?" Alex took a firmer hold.

Sass listened for another rumble, or a lightning flash, but the noise didn't recede; it was getting louder and coming toward them like a non-stop train through a station. Sass felt the ground shake ... and then shift – and slide. The earth was moving. She heard a scream. The terrified neigh of a horse as Bo reared up, only to be swallowed by a serpent of mud and rocks and water.

When the flood came, Alex instinctively scrambled backward, his heels digging in the ground.

"Sass, get back!" But his shout came too late as he watched her get swept away by the current. He'd hung on to Bo, but in her terror, the horse had gone up on her hind legs, desperate to be released. Pulled off his feet, his last image was of the falling animal, grey fading to black, as he too fell back and smacked his head hard on the ground. There was a brief hideous rush in his ears as he passed out cold.

When he came around again, minutes or maybe hours later, the sky above him still howled. His head throbbed and he was bleeding, the relentless rain filling his mouth and nose.

Sass.

Where was she?

Alex tried to get to his feet, but he couldn't move his legs. He swore. A dead weight that wouldn't shift was pinning them down. In a panic, he began scrabbling and somehow he managed to pull himself free from the wreckage of the trailer. He got to his hands and knees and vomited: rain, river and bitter bile.

"Sass!" His pathetic shout a cracked mess. He tried again. "Sass? Sass! Can you hear me?"

Adrenalin took over. He shouted again, and again, his heart pumping in his ears.

"Sass? Where are you? Answer me."

He looked around him, scanning the riverbank. The trailer had completely gone; the only place he'd ever felt safe, smashed up as if it had never existed. The creek, his creek, where he'd met her, was a torrent battering its way to the sea.

And Sass and Bo were nowhere to be found.

Dragged off her feet, Sass had twisted onto her belly and tried to grasp at anything to stop herself from being taken by the flood tide, but it was hopeless; she was fighting to stay alive in a whirlpool. She forgot about sadness and a life in rewind. The only thing she could think of was that she wasn't ready to die. This was not her time. She had everything to live for, didn't she? To love and be loved. If only she could breathe. Breathe, Sass. Breathe!

Banged and buffeted, the current took her. She tried to stay on the surface, but her boots and Alex's coat were dragging her down, and then came the terrible, choking, inevitable moment when her head went under, and she could see nothing but murk, her ears deafened to everything except the weird churn of water. Sass didn't know which way was up as she rolled and pitched and tumbled, over and over, until her lungs burst.

Sass swam for her life: it was that, or twist and die. With one last frantic effort, she wrestled with the river and bobbed up, spat out by the current, and with a huge gasp for air, she reached up and grasped at an overhanging branch that she clung to with all her strength. Hanging there with burning arms, her chin scraping bark, she shuddered with relief, hot tears running down her face.

She was alive, but where was Bo? And oh my god, Alex?

Sass stared across at the bank of the creek. It wasn't how she remembered it. How could this have happened so fast? She squinted harder. There in the mud on the shore was a figure. Was it him? Alex. Was he hurt? Was he dead? A sob rose in her throat. Then the body moved, painfully at first; doubled up over its knees.

"Alex?" she cried out, though she couldn't possibly be heard. "Alex!" she sobbed, her voice breaking. How could she reach him? Her arms were so, so tired.

From somewhere behind her came another low sound. The dull groan of an animal. Sass tore her eyes from the riverbank and turned her head to the uprooted tree that she was clinging to. Almost within touching distance, with the current between them, was Bo, trapped by trailing boughs that looked like the knotted hair of a drowned witch. The mare's face was bloodied and covered in mud, but Sass heard her whicker, her dark horse's eyes the only shining thing in the chaos.

"Bo? Hey, girl, I'm coming. Wait for me —" And Sass let go of her precious branch.

Alex blundered downstream, following the course of the water. How could half a ton of horse and a girl who could swim like a fish be washed away? "You'll have to catch me," came her voice in his mind, a tease that became a taunt. He squeezed his eyes shut and saw Sass swimming on her back, her long legs kicking. Taking a deep breath, he cried out once more into the darkness.

"Where you are you, Sass? Help me! Tell me where you are?" He stopped to listen.

Nothing. *Nothing!*

He pushed past uprooted trees and bushes. Began searching through the smashed remains of the trailer: planks of wood and torn metal, a washed-up sweater, Bo's old stable rug that he'd slept under the night he took off from school.

"Bo?" He cried out to the horse who'd taught him to ride, puke rising and sticking in his throat.

Alex fell for what felt like the hundredth time in the mud. Should he carry on searching, or go for help? How long would it take for him to return to the house? And then what? How could he even think of leaving while Sass and Bo were still out there?

But as he looked up at the sky, the choice wasn't hard. He

knew in his stomach, to the core of him, his very bones, that he'd keep on searching until he found them, because without Sass, he'd be ... what? Nothing. He scanned the dark water again, and in the corner of his eye, he caught a movement: a glint of light coming from a dam of twisted black roots and upturned bushes, maybe fifty yards or so downstream from where he stood. He staggered to the water's edge until he was directly opposite, squinting into the darkness; so hard to see or hear anything above the din of the water.

There. A glimmer of grey-white. Was that Bo?

Slicked with mud, the mare was almost ghostly, her eyes half closed, ears barely twitching, and next to her, chin deep in the still-rising current was ... Sass. Who was holding up whom, Alex couldn't tell, but they were alive.

"Sass!" His whisper a proper shout at last. "Hold on. You hear?"

Had she heard him? He'd no idea because he didn't wait. He dived into the water and began to swim.

Sass had made it to Bo, floundering like a kid without arm bands. She had scraped every last ounce of strength and gone to the horse because Bo needed her. They'd be better waiting together. She stroked the face of the mare, who, after rallying a little, had closed her eyes. Poor Bo; however cold and dizzy Sass felt, she'd stay with her.

From the water's edge came a shout. Sass looked up, but she couldn't see a thing. Then from out of the water came a face in the rain that she loved. Alex's voice lit her senses like a flame to her heart.

"Alex? *Alex!*"

He slid his arms beneath hers and she wrapped herself around him, and buried her face in his neck.

"I've got you, Sass. Don't you dare let go!" "I won't. Oh, Alex. I won't."

"I'm so glad you're okay." His voice broke. "I love you, Sass."

"Alex, I love you too." Her head so heavy on his shoulder that she could barely lift it.

"Listen, Sass." Alex was speaking to her again, "We have to get to the shore and then I can go for help."

"We can't leave Bo. She's in pain."

He tilted her chin to his. His face was so pale and cold.

"We have to leave her, Sass, but I'll return for her, I promise."

When he took her face in his hands and kissed her cheek, blood, rain, and tears washed over his wrists.

Alex steadfastly refused to look at Bo. He couldn't bear to. The horse who had given him everything.

"Sass, we have to go now."

"*No!* I won't leave her."

He touched Sass's cut face and gently stroked the water from her hair, his hand moving from Sass's head to Bo's neck. The girl and horse were as one. He took hold of Bo's trailing reins. He had to save them both or die trying.

"Come on, Bo — walk on." He gave the command that he'd used a million times. Bo gave a shuddering lurch and Alex was afraid that if she began to kick out, they'd all drown. He also knew that she had to fight her way out. He put the reins over her head and smoothed her slicked neck.

"Sass, get on her back."

"No. She's too weak."

"Get on her back, or we leave her." He wasn't asking Sass, he was telling her.

"How can I?"

"Because I say so, and it's what she understands. It's her best chance." And he hoisted Sass on. "Now ask her to move. Use your legs — hard. And your voice."

He slapped the mare's neck with the reins, his teeth gritted.

The mare gave a huge heave, her hooves finding some sort of foothold on the riverbed.

"Now, Sass, steer her for the shore. Kick her on." And Alex hung on by the bridle and Bo's tail, and kicked out for himself.

Somewhere above the coursing water, he became conscious of the faint whine of a siren, followed by a flash of blue at the top of the meadow, as a police 4x4 and a fire rescue truck ploughed and skidded their way down to them. Shouts from the paddock were swallowed by darkness, replaced by bobbing torches, and above them came the throbbing rotor blades of a search helicopter, its arc of light cutting through the wreckage.

Sass knelt in the mud and dead leaves at the water's edge and stroked the crest of Bo's neck. Even after a rescuer had carried her away, she looked back over a burly shoulder and reached out. Then with her eyes tight shut, pain in every jolting movement, she felt herself taken to safety. More arms took her; she couldn't seem to stand, her knees giving way when her legs wouldn't work, like a puppet on a string. She was laid on a stretcher, her head in some sort of vice, a tight mask placed across her face. Someone was with her, she half recognized, but it wasn't Mom. Who was it? She couldn't see. Suddenly she wanted her mom. "Mom!" There was a sharp prick in her arm and then everything went blurry, and the pain in her body became a heartache that in turn became a fuzzy nothing. Where was her silver horse; had someone saved her? And where was Alex now? In her mind, he held her hand, but he wasn't by her side. Was he with Bo? She hoped so. She just needed to rest her eyes, her head was so . . . so tired.

39

LANDSLIDE

When Alex first ran out of the house, Helena had waited in the drawing room. She didn't like to make a fuss and had been certain that Alex would find Saskia quickly. They deserved a private moment together.

Four hours had since passed and the light, and the weather, had deteriorated. With a heavy heart, Helena had made the call to James Harrison, Alex's new policeman, who was staying in the lodge. Until now, Trist had been the one place he didn't need round-the-clock protection. Wherever Alex was, she needed him found. Call it the jitters, but a lump of fear was growing in her stomach. She leaned against a chair with the receiver to her ear, her legs trembling. Water leaked in at the base of the French windows, seeping along the old oak floor and staining the silk curtains that pooled on the ground. Above her, the painted foam horses back in their place above the mantelpiece plunged through the waves, the whites of their eyes a warning through the spray.

Unable to sit, Helena went down to the yard for news, only to find the horses ill at ease, and the drains overflowing. Dancer was kicking at his door and Figgy and Amy stood in a knot whispering to the capable young farrier, Dan.

Figgy spoke first. Dear Figgy.

"Have you called for help, Your Ladyship?" Her forehead crumpled with concern.

"Yes, but Alex will return soon — you'll see; he just needs a chance to find her."

But then, in the not-so-far distance, came a boom, a sound that she dreaded to hear again. The roaring of a plane with its engines screaming and on fire. Except it wasn't a plane and this wasn't the war, and the ground was shaking beneath her feet. It was the crack and shudder of a hillside sliding toward the sea.

Landslide.

Helena swayed on her feet and Figgy caught her by the elbow.

A voice she barely recognized as her own cried shrilly.

"Dear lord! Call 999, call the coastguard, call the whole damn lot, if Alex and Saskia are caught up in this!"

Like every small boy, Alex had liked to roam, and of course he'd had a den. Alex was no different from other children, whatever was said. His hiding place was the ancient horsebox tucked down beside the creek, where they'd once stored winter feed and hay. Had he gone there to find her? She let out a long, tremulous sigh: the summer meadow, where every Tremayne went to hide, rest and play ... and to fall in love. Nowhere more perfect, until now.

Helena wasn't praying; she'd given up on prayer a long time ago. It was a turn of phrase, that was all, a habit that died hard. She held herself erect. She'd seen fire and now here was the flood; she'd not crumble, however biblically awful. Her mind turned to Saskia. Her uncle had to be informed; she'd send Corbett at once. Was she unnecessarily panic-stricken; was she entirely mistaken? She hoped so, she desperately did, but some instinct, some sixth sense, told her otherwise.

40

SAYING GOODBYE

After Sass was safe, Alex threw off the strong arms that took his. Who cared about him when Bo was lying in the mud half dead? He refused to be a useless spectator. Jim was there, on the radio barking information, and a vet he didn't recognize had arrived.

What were they doing that could take so long? An animal-rescue fire truck was being reversed, its winch exposed with a giant hanging cradle. Alex knelt beside Bo in the sludge. Was she breathing? Let her still be breathing. Alex took the horse's head in his lap and stroked the length of her jaw. She made a low sound; Bo knew he was there, though her eyes stayed closed, her flanks barely moving, her tail a limp flag of surrender.

The vet bent to her task. She was young, doing emergency out of hours. He heard her talking to Jim and Dan. Dan was a good bloke; treated Alex like a friend.

"I want to put her out of her misery. Who do I ask?"

"You can't do it," answered Dan, "the horse means too much to him."

"Can't you save her?"

"Look at the mare. She's broken; it's not fair."

Alex watched Dan stand up and run a hand through his fair hair. Someone had given him a neon jacket that he'd half pulled over his clothes. He crouched down beside Alex, who knew already what he was going to say.

"Alex. You know what's right. Her Ladyship will understand." "No!" Alex shocked himself at the violence of his reaction.

Bo's eyelids flickered. "No, I won't let you. She's a fighter; give her a chance."

Dan turned to him, put both hands on his shoulders.

"Alex, you understand horses. This is not about chances, it's about doing what's right for her. She's an old horse and suffering badly ... Say goodbye."

Alex nodded blindly. He shut his eyes; he wasn't ashamed of his tears. This horse had shown him so much. Given him everything. In his head, Sass whispered, "She's so beautiful. Is she yours?" The voice he couldn't ignore.

It took seconds.

"It's done, she's gone..." the young vet whispered, putting the syringe away: professional, but visibly shaken.

"It was the right thing," Dan murmured, his hand on Alex's shoulder.

Helena was driven by Figgy as close to the creek as possible. She had forgotten her mackintosh and shook a little when she saw the scene. It was like the stage set of a tragic opera: the fire brigade, police, and a veterinarian she didn't know were all assembled in luminous yellow in the gathering darkness.

In the time it had taken for an old woman to struggle across a field, an ambulance had left with Saskia on board. Helena had been told at the house that both were safe, but where was Alex? She looked around fearfully. Had he gone to hospital too? She needed to know. And where was Bo? The marc hadn't galloped home. She felt so very responsible and yet suddenly so terribly frail.

She looked across the surging water and saw her grandson kneeling on the bank: her summer meadow splayed wide. What was he doing on his knees? Something was cradled in his arms. She stumbled closer. The day had almost gone, while the moon cowered in the sky.

When Sass had run out at lunchtime, David had let her go. If she needed time by herself, who was he to stop her? — but as the weather got worse, he couldn't concentrate. He'd grabbed his car keys and headed to the estate, the most obvious place she'd have gone.

At the house, the grim-faced butler told him what had happened. A million things went through his mind as he reversed the Land Rover back around and stepped on the accelerator, the 4x4 straining up the drive in a cloud of smoking rubber. He clenched the wheel, skidding in a shower of spray and somewhere before the main gates he leapt out and flagged down a departing ambulance and police escort, praying that Sass was on board alive and well.

At the hospital, she was out of it, murmuring drugged nonsense to herself. David held her hand as he'd done that one time not long after she was born, her tiny hands squeezed into tiny pink fists. Fighting fists. He looked at her long fingers now, her skin almost transparent from the water, her nails torn from holding on.

He thought of his big sister, and how she had died. Those photos. Had it been instant? Or was he comforting himself? He thought of the lost years and the pain he must have caused when he left. He should've stayed, because there was one last truth he had to tell Sass, if she got through all this. Laura was not her mother — not her natural mother, though his sister had raised her as if she was. What did it take for her to raise a child by herself? A child who wasn't her own, but his. His daughter with a girl he met whose face he'd forgotten until he saw what they'd made, nine months later. He felt a shudder run through him as something inside of him split and the tears rolled down his face. He rubbed them away. Sass no longer had a mother, but sixteen years on, he could step up and be the father she'd never had.

41

A BRUISED ANGEL

"Alex?" Sass whispered, her eyes still closed. His name the only clearness in her head. It hurt to take a breath, as if a steamroller had squashed her flat. Her favourite kindergarten teacher, Mrs Hull, with the wriggly hair and the beautiful handwriting, had read a story once about a kid who could slide under doors, and mail himself to friends. Flat Stanley. She felt like him.

A change in the air, and her bed shifted. "Sass, open your eyes."

She made herself open them. And smiled. Alex was leaning over her. He took her hand.

"Sass. You're safe in the hospital. Here with me."

She blinked back sleepily.

Then she remembered. Struggled to sit up.

"Bo?"

Alex's face clouded, and Sass knew then. Just as she'd

known when the doctor had told her about Mom. It was the way the man twisted his hands in his white-coat pocket. She'd made him say it three times, poor guy, because hard stuff made you stupid. You had to hear it again and again.

"Say it?" she whispered to Alex.

"Sass..." He kissed her face. "Bo's gone. We couldn't save her. I was with her the whole time and she wasn't in pain at the end."

A monitor bleeped as Alex bent to kiss Sass's forehead, careful not to put any more weight on her body. A bruised angel in a hospital gown. He looked past the black eye and the stitches across her nose. Sass had never looked more beautiful. When he straightened up, he saw her face was wet with tears.

"Say it again?" She was crying quietly. Her shoulder and arm bandaged by her side. He stopped the tears on her cheek with his finger. "It was nobody's fault. We tried but we couldn't help her." A whisper to himself. And all of a sudden, he was crying too, gulping and blubbing like a baby.

They were still hugging when his parents came to find him. They'd flown down in the night — together. He hadn't expected that. And they'd faced the press together this morning. He blocked the distant clamour outside. His father coughed politely.

"I see you've found each other. Alex, we don't want to interrupt, but just to say, we'll be back tomorrow before you go home — to Trist."

His eyes spoke volumes; his father had understood at last.

Amy was a wheel spinning in mud. Sludge filled her head with a thick layer of guilt. She walked down to the paddock where Dancer was grazing in the sunshine that followed the storm. He'd rolled. He always rolled and it caked his sides, cracking where it had begun to dry. She'd need to wash him down, scrub it off by the look of it. Above her, gulls cried in a sky so blue that she could almost forget what had happened. If she could just keep her face turned up to it; the gulls made a din every day at this time, following the fishing boats out in the bay. She hadn't much noticed them until now. All the little things that were part of her day: the stiff catch of the field gate that trapped her fingers if she wasn't careful dragging it open; the trudge over to check the horses' water trough, the walk back to the stables, to the hay-nets she'd filled earlier. All the little things that meant she was sometimes bored, but still happy.

Bo was no more. She was dead. How many times had Amy ridden to the meadow on Dancer to check the mare was all good while Alex was at school? Alexander. His Royal Highness. Like he was on high and she was what — so low? He wouldn't be Alex to her anymore. He was never her Alex — she knew that. She'd never see him again, except on TV or the like. If she'd passed on the note, then they might've stayed friends. That stupid scribbled note in his not-posh handwriting. If she'd been nicer to the girl herself — Sass who'd sucked up attention from everyone: the Countess, Figgy — from Alex, that made her so, so jealous after Plum.

Well — the girl nearly drowned. Alex too. And it was her — Amy's — fault. Too many ifs. Well, if stiffed. If she'd made it right between them like she was supposed to, then Bo would still be here.

Amy still had a bit of packing to do. She was leaving. The Countess didn't know she was going, nor did Figgy, but she had to do this to make it right. She'd bring Dancer in, wash him down for the last time, whisper goodbye to Bo in her empty stable, then collect her stuff from the tackroom. The note itself was safe. She'd ironed it flat where it got a bit damp, and curled at the edges, and stuck it in an envelope that she left on the hall table in the big house with "Alex" on the front in thick felt-tip. He could give it to Sass himself when they got back from the hospital later. On her way out, she'd touched the head of the small, rough-done horse sculpture she'd once seen the Countess touch "for luck".

Dan was coming in his van. She'd told him everything and he hadn't judged her. He'd put in a good word at another stable he went to. They'd sat in the old hay barn and he'd handed her his bottle of water while she blubbed. She'd tried not to swig it all. The curve of his shoulder was so broad through his tee-shirt that she'd have liked to have crept closer and rested her head there. He smelled of hoof oil and charcoal. His hands were big and strong, and calloused, and warm. Dan wasn't hers either, but maybe from his steady gaze he could be. One day. Maybe. "Time is a healer," he said.

42

GOING HOME

Helena leaned on Corbett as he and a uniformed police officer manhandled her through the massed press outside the hospital. She tried to ignore the barrage of shouts and camera flashes; she'd rather hoped they'd all have left after Seraphina and the prince made their statement about Alexander yesterday.

No. It seemed they wanted more.

"What can you tell us about the prince and his girl?" So discourteous.

"When are they coming out?" So rude.

"Are the prince and princess getting back together again?" Quite ridiculous.

And one particularly vile question from a jaded-looking hag Helena faintly recognized.

"Was it her that Prince Alex was caught out with? Our tragic holiday girl?"

Helena stopped. That woman was offensive on almost

every level. She gave her a stare that could wither grapes on a vine; raisin-faced, the creature stepped back.

Helena made her way into the hospital and, with the help of Corbett, soon found Saskia's room. Alexander was sitting on Saskia's bed; sweet but hardly appropriate. They were coming home today. To Trist, to be precise. It was agreed that Helena could offer them somewhere to recover away from the world's prying eyes. Extra security had been drafted in. Poor girl, there would be more press, but at least she could be sheltered until the vultures moved on.

Helena cast her mind back to the dark days of her scandal. 1943. Even then, it had made the papers. They called her "The Pin-Up" for falling for a married airman. When her light-hearted cowboy had plunged his plane into the sea, she'd had no one: she had been utterly heartbroken.

"Grandma! Come in."

Alex grinned up at her. Helena cupped his chin and patted Sass's good hand.

"How are we today?"

"Coming home. We're not staying in here any longer, are we, Sass?"

"I see you're both ready. Be sure to thank everyone."

"Grandma — please."

"Corbett is waiting with the car. There's quite a crush outside. Are you listening, Alexander?"

Sass was distracted by the arrival of the extra security; she had no idea of what was coming, though the hospital reception area was the first clue. It was like an explosion in a florist's shop, with an entire wall devoted to get-well cards. His and hers. It was . . . kind of odd.

After handshakes with the hospital staff, she and Alex stepped outside, where a black Range Rover stood parked with its engine running and the doors open. From beyond the main gates, she could hear the faint sound of cheering.

Sass sank into her seat, her left arm now in plaster, her shoulder well strapped. As the car made its cautious exit, a surge of people came forward. She shrank back. Who were they?

Alex, by contrast, sat forward. His leg jiggled next to hers, but he was smiling and nodding so much that Sass just wanted to hunch out of sight.

"What are you doing?" she asked.

"All these people have been waiting to wish us well for the last few days. We can't just sneak out the back. It's nothing, it's just waving."

Alex glanced across at her, his eyes intense, looking for a sign that she understood. Sass didn't, not even for him.

The car crept forward, joined by Helena in the old Bentley behind and a flashing police escort, and they were about to move off when Alex did something that Sass would never forget.

He opened the door.

"Alex, no!" She cried.

The car slammed to a halt. Alex leapt out, swiftly followed by his bodyguard, only for them both to be swallowed by a whole crush of people. Sass watched as, awkwardly at first,

Alex smiled and shook hands. Soon he was waving with both hands and working the crowd. He strode forward, posed for selfies, and ruffled babies' hair, his policeman, Jim, beside him, muttering into a tiny mouthpiece.

Sass sat rigid, hoping that no one would notice her sitting in the corner of the car.

A small girl did.

The girl tapped on the window of Alex's hastily slammed door and waved a posy of flowers. Sass smiled politely as the child tried to tell her something. With difficulty, Sass slid across the seat to Alex's side and rolled down the window, her good hand cupped to her ear. The child wriggled her way around to the front.

"Are you a princess?" she asked, thrusting the flowers in Sass's face.

"No, but don't tell anyone. Are you?"

"Nah, don't be silly."

"Are these for me? They're lovely."

"Yes, I picked them in Granny's garden. My name's Lizzie. Lizzie Bunnage. I'm six."

"Wow, six? I'm sixteen. Almost. Is that for me too?" She pointed at a hand-drawn card that Lizzie was holding.

"It's for the hurt on your face." She pointed at Sass's stitches.

"Thank you, that's sweet. The hurt's getting better. I'm Sass, by the way." She leaned forward and whispered it in Lizzie's ear.

The child beamed. "That tickled."

Sass smiled. It was true; she was still herself. She was

okay. It tickled. And this little kid meant her no harm, just the opposite. She made Sass feel good inside.

Alex fought his way back to the car and opened the door. He caught Sass's hand and pulled her gently to him, keeping her close. He murmured in her ear and kissed her on the temple to the cheers of the crowd.

One final wave and then they were ushered back by bodyguards. They were done; the crowds parted and the motorcade rolled away. Sass breathed out, a long, long sigh, and rested her head by the window as the leaf-green blur rushed by.

She was soon fast asleep.

Alex watched her. A loose strand of hair was sticking to her bottom lip. Her skin was so pale now that he could join the dots that freckled her nose. The cut was beginning to heal over, stitched with tiny spider-like blue threads. He imagined a nurse deciding on the colour. He reached down and picked up her hand: "Good waving, girl," he murmured, kissing the sore knuckles.

No "exclusive" either for Cressida Slater. If she was out there somewhere, she wasn't making money this time, because every other photo just now would be better. He'd won this round in the ring. Alex leaned back in his seat. It wasn't much of a victory, but a charge of energy flowed through him. This was a game he could play. His whole life stretched ahead. Sure, he needed his space, he needed fresh air, but he could do this now, he knew it. Not the old way, but maybe in his way.

The crunch of gravel woke Sass from her nap. The car was pulling up. She looked out the window and saw a long shadow lift from the face of the house, as the cloud made way for the sun. Trist was a sight she would never take for granted.

David and Jessie stood on the front steps waiting. Helena had explained about the need for extra security till the end of the summer. They'd understood, Sass hoped. She sat up and peered closer, her heart bumping; was that Harry by David's feet? She got out of the car and the dog shot straight towards her. With a gulp and a smile, Sass folded herself into a one-armed family-sized hug.

In a grand room, Corbett set down afternoon tea on top of a huge, squishy footstool that Helena called an ottoman. Sass smiled at David, who winked and murmured that it could "fit a-lot-o-men". On the tray was a silver teapot; five china cups and saucers; a pot of sugar lumps with a tiny pair of tongs; and a sort of carousel of sandwiches and sponge cake. It didn't take long to eat it, but all too soon it was time for Jessie and David to leave. They'd be back tomorrow for the birthday Sass had almost forgotten.

Alex reached for her hand.

"Come with me," he whispered, "there's something I want to show you."

"Oh?"

He tugged her past the yard. Neither of them yet ready to face Bo's empty box.

"One last thing that I've been keeping from you. Not in the secretive sense; it just never came up at the right time. Grandma was going to show you, but what with —" He frowned and toyed with her hand.

He took her through a painted-brick archway that Sass had always assumed led to where the gardener, a crusty old guy named Roberts, kept his stuff. Her hand traced the yellowing stone that whispered of olden times; past cobwebby flowerpots, a neatly coiled hosepipe and a pair of chipped green watering cans. All the way through to an enclosed, walled garden.

Once a place to grow flowers or vegetables, it was now a pen of ankle-deep grass: the perfect place of safety for a pair of ... foals!

The two looked up, ears pricked. They jostled closer. The braver one was almost smoke blue and snorted down her nose like a baby dragon. The silver buckle on her tiny head collar glinted in the late afternoon light. The second was the colour of tealeaves, bashful as he snuck in behind his girlfriend.

Alex ducked under the gate and went over to them.

"Hello, you two. I've brought someone to meet you." Alex scratched behind their ears. Stumpy tails flicked appreciatively.

"They're beautiful..." Sass's spirits rose. She reached out her open palm to the nearest one.

"They're the reason you found Bo in the summer meadow."

"What do you mean?"

"The dark grey nuzzling your hand is her foal, born seven months ago. Grandma had been weaning her, giving her mother, Bo, the summer off."

"A foal? I had no idea. You never said."

"There are so many things I should have said earlier." Alex stubbed the toe of his boot in the ground.

"But wasn't it awful, to separate them?"

"They're horses, Sass, not humans."

"Still —"

"It's fine. It's nature and she's got a friend."

Sass turned to Bo's foal and patted her mane, a thick, fluffy ruff of black.

"She doesn't look like her mother. She's not nearly as white."

"She'll lighten. She already moves like a dream. Look at her clean, straight limbs."

"She's all big ears and feet to me."

"Too right. But she's got it all. You wait."

Bo's filly was the more alert of the two. Beautiful and yet it seemed to Sass that the foal's shining eyes were mirrors of sadness that the foal couldn't possibly feel. Could she?

The youngster answered her with a naughty squeal and a pirouette, her tail whisking like a feather duster. Sass was pleased. She was bright-eyed, not sad-eyed after all. Sass looked across at Alex, who was leaning against the gate with his head down, his face hidden for a few private moments. Sensing her, he looked sideways.

"What would you call her if she were yours?"

"Bo's foal?"

"Yes."

"How about … Bucky? Gem? Munchie or Fruit Loop?" Anything to make him feel better.

"You *are* joking?" A half smile.

She answered with a small nod.

"What do you think of…"

"Go on…" said Sass.

Alex paused. "Well, you know the saying, every black cloud has a —?"

"Silver lining," she finished. "I like it. I mean, I really like it. What will your grandmother say?"

"I don't know. It's not too gloomy, is it?"

"No, it's perfect, but she'll have to have a nickname." "Think of one, then."

"How about Summer? Storm would be right, but a summer is what Bo has given us. A happy time," she said firmly. "I guess that's what the saying means."

"Then Summer it is. And there's another reason I've brought you here. After Grandma got to know you, before all this, she wanted to … And I know it's a day early, but — Summer's your sixteenth birthday present."

Alex took her hands and shook them out. Sass couldn't speak, her heart was so full.

"Do you think we can be happy again?" Alex asked. "Sure I do…"

There was no other choice.

He bumped his forehead to hers. "Then — I do too."

43

CANDLE LIGHT

The day was fading when Alex took her back to the house. He said it would soon be time for dinner, but first, he wanted her all to himself.

In the old servants' basement, he kissed her. They kissed again in the scullery. He kissed her in the boot room and against the wall of the pantry that led to the kitchen where he stole matches and a silver candlestick, and led her upstairs.

Half walking, half running, he tugged her hand down the long corridor to the closed-off double doors at the end.

"Where are we going?" she asked, her voice quickening in the darkness.

"To see the house by candlelight. The way it was meant to be seen."

With fumbling fingers, Alex struck a match, which flared as it touched the wick of the candle. When he pushed open the doors, Sass heard herself gasp as the quivering light curled over scarlet-silk walls and cornices of twisted gold.

At a window, Alex pulled apart drawn velvet curtains, and they gazed past their reflections all the way to the sea. It felt like the cloak of England was laid out before her.

Alex spun her around gently. He was pointing up at a wall of pictures, his hand tight at her waist.

"Meet my less famous family."

Sass gazed up. Long faces looked down. Kind of haughty. All except one.

"That's your grandmother? She looks so young." Sass thought of the Helena she knew with the same sharp eyes and unmistakable cheekbones. She tilted her head to look more closely. There was a flush to the face, an anticipation, unless it was a trick of the flame? She wondered if Helena's foot tapped as she sat for the artist.

Alex read her mind.

"Some scandal broke not long after this was painted; we never talk of it."

"Don't you want to know?" Sass knew *she* would.

"Of course, but it's private. Anyway, it was way back during the war."

Sass remembered her own conversation with the Countess: "Secrecy is so much more exciting." Why did she say that? And was it good or bad? Were secrets so innermost that you hugged them to you, or was the opposite true; it was the risk of being found out that made them feel so dangerously good?

A glint caught her eye: this time a crystal-framed wedding photo on a side table. Sass reached over and picked it up.

"These are my parents." Alex continued, "You met them at the hospital."

It looked like the fanciest wedding possible. She almost dropped it. A royal wedding. Alex's father stood stiff-backed in uniform while his mother shone in a pool of silver lace, clutching a vast bouquet of roses, her flower girls trailing adorably. A tiara sparkled in her upswept hair.

Alex pulled at her sleeve.

"Listen, this isn't me, or what I would choose, but it's what I have to become. It is my duty, I suppose."

"But not now," Sass whispered, squeezing his hand.

"Not now." He smiled. "One day."

Alex took her upstairs, to the door of the bedroom beneath his own. There were sixteen others he could have chosen, but this was the closest that Grandma would allow. Just a floor between them, when all he wanted was to hear her breathing.

Downstairs in the hall, the old grandfather clock struck seven.

Sass gazed around the room. "Alex — it's beautiful. The walls — they're painted twilight."

Alex laughed. "It's not the grandest room, but it's not too shabby. It gets the sun at the end of the day and it's near to you; just a layer of plaster and floorboards away."

"That's true, I'll hear you sleep-talking."

"Snoring, more like."

And Sass leaned in and hugged him until he was afraid that she'd break.

He reached inside his pocket for the giftbox. "Got you something when I was in London."

Her face lit up. "You did? What is it?"

"Open it and see."

She sat cross-legged on the four-poster bed and picked the box up. She put it down. She held it to her ear like a seashell and gave it a little rattle. Mom used to drive her crazy unwrapping gifts, she was so slow. She'd take her time, keeping the bow "for another occasion", even smoothing out the discarded wrapping, like there was no hurry.

Tugging at the white ribbon, she tore off the teal-coloured paper until she was left with the naked box. She paused: the words "TIFFANY & CO" were printed on top. What? Audrey Hepburn's Tiffany? A little squeak escaped her: New York, London, Paris and Rome. A tingle of excitement that started in her toes and ended in her fingertips. She lifted the clamshell lid, and resting against the velvet was a silver horseshoe on a chain.

Alex helped her to put it on as she sat at an old-fashioned, bean-shaped dressing table swathed in a misty-coloured silk that was tattered in places. She touched her throat where he'd kissed her. She would wear the necklace tonight. Not that it could alter how she looked.

In the looking glass, Wolf Girl had been in a fight. A big one. And lost. She glared at the cuts and grazes, held up her loose hair, and looked left and right.

Alex caught her eye in the mirror. His black eye had turned yellow. They out-gazed each other until he looked away first. She laughed. She'd won, but he made her feel lighter than the air that she sometimes still struggled to breathe.

"Listen, I'm out of here, before Grandma catches me. Okay?"

"Wait." She turned around. "What am I going to wear tonight?"

He grinned.

"How should I know? It's almost your birthday. Wear nothing." A devilish grin. "Or take a look in there?" He nodded at the double doors of a closet behind her.

"Can I?"

"Sure, it's bound to be full of Mum's stuff."

"I couldn't —"

"Come on, she won't mind. She never wears half of it. Go on, do it, now."

And he left her and went out.

Sass opened the walk-in wardrobe. Oh my god, she was halfway to Narnia. She almost expected a talking fawn to fall out in high heels. There were dresses on velvet-padded hangers: in cotton, silk, linen and lace. More soft colours than a box of sugar-dusted Turkish delight. How could anyone know what was in here, let alone what to choose?

In the end, she didn't have to because the dress chose itself. A sheer silk and lace slip rustled to the ground, the colour of a blush. Would it fit, did she dare? It was almost backless, with two thin straps that crossed between her shoulder blades. So . . . grown up. So perfect.

Wriggling it on, Sass looked again in the mirror. It fit her frame as if it were made for her.

There was a knock on the door: a sharp *rat-a-tat-tat*.

"May I come in?" It was Helena.

"Yes, of course." She opened the door wide.

Helena stood, elegant in wide trousers and a black velvet stole.

"My dear, I see you've found something lovely." The Countess's eyes took her in. "Have you everything you need? A little cardigan, perhaps?"

She glanced from Sass and surveyed the rest of the room, her eyes resting on the discarded gift wrap. She bent stiffly and picked up the crushed ribbon.

"That was her name, you know?" Helena said sadly. "What was?"

"Silver Ribbon."

"I'm sorry, I don't follow."

"Bo's proper name; her race name was Silver Ribbon. I shortened it to Bo. Her stable name, you see?"

Sass felt her heart beat faster. She reached for the photograph of her great-grandpa lounging against his plane.

"Who's that?" Helena asked, stepping closer, her voice rising slightly.

"It's an old photo; my Uncle David packed it with my things. It's of my great-grandfather and his crew. I wanted to show you. He was here in Cornwall during the war. You know, like you said that day in the churchyard? He was an American airman, an officer pilot. His name was Jack Rigby."

"I see. . ." But Helena was all confusion, her lined face filled with a sort of anguished longing. "There were so many Jacks, my dear, and most of them died. I can't possibly remember them all."

"Won't you take another look?"

Helena put her hand out to sit down on the bed. Sass reached across and put the frame in her lap.

"Please? You see, David says Jack Rigby might have been billeted here at Trist. Maybe — you even met him once?"

Sass felt the lightest lift and fall in the air of the room; a gentle flow that heated her inside and out. She had the strangest feeling that something extraordinary had, or was about to happen.

Helena picked up the frame with shaking hands. She knew this photograph, or rather, the boys in it. It must have gone home with his things. The greatest love of her life was staring back at her from here in this room.

Saskia was his great-granddaughter. Helena shook her head.

How could fate strike twice?

She hadn't meant to fall for Jack: he was married with a baby on the way, but it had happened anyway. She was only eighteen to his nineteen. Chalk and cheese, except when it came to horses. War made people behave differently; when one of you might die, you lived for the day, especially if you were young and headstrong, and so full of life. It was years before she could think about another man after Jack.

"There's something else," Saskia was saying. "Tucked behind the photo. Take a look?"

A silver ribbon fell out. Helena picked it up, smoothing it with her thumb. The tie that Jack had stolen from her hair the night he flew away. She let it slip through her fingers: watched it uncoil, its glittering threads twirling back time in the lamplight. He'd kept it. Even though he'd died, the past had framed a way to tell her, to remind her, that she had once been truly cherished.

Helena glanced up at Saskia and composed her face: years of practice mustered in a single sentence; English to the end.

"Perhaps I could keep the photograph for later? I may remember something."

She returned to the present and leaned across to Saskia.

"My dear, I think you need some help with your hair. What are we going to do with this?"

Half an hour later, from the shadow of the dining room, she watched her grandson's face as the girl he adored came down the stairs dressed in silk and lace, her hair swept up, a hint of cherry gloss on her lips and a pair of red-sequinned slippers on her feet. Helena peered closer: tied in a bow at Saskia's throat was a shining horseshoe on a frayed grey satin ribbon. And in the girl's soft tread on the step, it seemed to Helena that in one silver summer, what the skies had taken away, the sea had brought back.

ACKNOWLEDGEMENTS

It has only taken twenty-five years in children's publishing to write this book, so there are a few people who I must thank.

To Mum for joining me in the Puffin Club; for opening a school bookshop in a far-flung school, so that books never ran out; and for reading (almost) every version of this manuscript. To Dad for taking me, as a little girl, to the library and for occasionally losing me there. To Sax and Rich "in loco parentis" and my brother, David, for turning out less annoying. For Ann, Bob, and Mark, my other family. To Little Tim, Gobbolino, Laura Ingalls and Nancy Drew for making me want to read. Then later, Roger McGough, Roald Dahl, Posy Simmonds and Jilly Cooper for being my literary heroes.

To Barry Cunningham, my boss and friend, for not giving me my first job, but the second, and my time with the Coop. To all the Chickens for reading this, but especially Rachel Leyshon for "ironing out the wrinkles" and Her Ladyship Helena Bagenal. To a brilliant editor, Mallory Kass at Scholastic, for loving horses, and for shining such a thoughtful light on this narrative, and to Ellie Berger for giving me the chance. To Helen Crawford-White for the beautiful cover art. And to my UK publisher, Ruth Huddleston, for being similarly horse- and book-minded.

To all my friends who didn't know they were lending me their surnames: Katie, Fiona, Penny, Carolyn, Karen, Philippa and Alison. To my god-daughters, nieces and first readers:

Izzie P, Lizzie B, the Warren sisters, Francesca, Sacha, Chloe and Jess. To Sarah, Lisa, Chris and Nadine for sharing in the horses.

Finally and most important of all: Simon "HH", who has always believed in me. My children, Jack, Harry and Isobel Lily (named for the granny who made up stories about Carlo the dog). And the four-legged troupe: the dastardly Mac, immaculate Munch and silver baby Marble.